The Forgotten Song

Richard Clark

Praise for Richard Clark's Books

'*The Forgotten Song* is an entirely captivating tale from cover to cover.'

Patricia Wilson, bestselling author of *Island of Secrets, Villa of Secrets, Secrets of Santorini* and *Greek Island Escape*

'Clark is particularly good on the colours, flavours and scents of Greece. He has got under the skin of the place in a way few outsiders have been able to.'

Mark Hudson, winner of *Somerset Maugham Award, Thomas Cook Travel Book Award, Samuel Johnson Prize*

Richard Clark captures the spirit of Greece I love. His books make me long to see the places he describes.'

Jennifer Barclay, author of *Falling in Honey, An Octopus in My Ouzo* and *Wild Abandon*

'There is poetry in Richard Clark's words and through his eyes. I recommend anyone missing Greece, visiting Greece or just wishing they could go to Greece to take a look!'

Sara Alexi, author of *The Greek Village Series*

By the Same Author

The Lost Lyra

Return to Turtle Beach

The Greek Islands – A Notebook

Crete – A Notebook

Rhodes – A Notebook

Corfu – A Notebook

Hidden Crete – A Notebook

More Hidden Crete – A Notebook

Eastern Crete – A Notebook

Richard Clark's Greek Islands Anthology

The Crete Trilogy

About the Author

Richard Clark is a writer, editor and journalist who has worked on an array of national newspapers and magazines in the UK. In 1982, on a whim, he decided to up sticks and live on the Greek island of Crete. So began a love affair that has continued to this day, and he still visits the Greek islands, where he has a home, on a regular basis. In 2016, he gave up the daily commute to London to become a full-time author. He is married with two grown up children and three grandchildren, and lives in Kent.

Acknowledgements

This book is a work of fiction, and although some real places have leant themselves as locations many are the product of my imagination and all the characters are fictitious, any resemblance to real persons, living or dead, is purely coincidental. Any mistakes are mine.

A huge thank you goes to Tony and Bernadette Prouse for reading each chapter as it was produced and for their guidance. I am also grateful to the author Yvonne Payne for reading and giving her comments on the final manuscript.

As always it has been a privilege to be edited by the wonderful Jennifer Barclay whose keen eye and friendly encouragement have made this book so much better than it otherwise might have been. Once again I am grateful to Mike Parsons for his exquisite illustrations for the cover. Last but not least I must thank my family, Denise, Rebecca, James, Pete, Lucy, Esther, Imogen and Iris for their unending support.

Note

The names of male Greek characters ending in an 's' will drop the letter in the vocative case (when that character is being addressed in direct speech).

For Denise

Prologue

PHOEBE MANAGED TO banish a pang of guilt as she looked out onto the olive grove. She smiled as she saw the children playing hide and seek while Andreas tended his brightly-coloured hives in the shade of the silver trees. It was the first day of the lockdown to try and halt the virus that was sweeping the world.

In the boy she could see his father; even at ten years old he was strong and carefree as he ran amongst the spring flowers carpeting the field. The girl, just one year his junior, asked more questions of the world, pausing the game to sit and wonder at a poppy or a bee.

The phone call had put her mind at rest. Her mother was well. Isolation in the cottage in Wiltshire would be no hardship for Liz.

In her mum's voice she sensed the joy, in spite of the sombre threat which hung in the air, their chat about getting necessities and how she was sad not to be able to get to Crete. It hadn't taken long for Elizabeth to reveal the source of her happiness.

'I've just heard our song on the radio. They said it is number fourteen in the download charts.' Elizabeth could not disguise her delight.

'Mum, that's brilliant!' It was hard for Phoebe to believe what she was hearing.

'Thank you so much darling, for everything. After all these years…' Tears of emotion welled up in Phoebe's eyes as her mother gushed.

'They say it is their "Record of the Week" and will play it on every show for the next seven days. Can you imagine?'

Out on the terrace Phoebe looked down the mountainside to the sea. Through a valley cut by some long-dried-out river she could see a triangle of blue glistening in the spring sunshine. In the garden, shoots of young vegetables, green and healthy, were bursting through the soil as the bells of their small flock of goats tinkled on the hillside.

Conflicted, Phoebe couldn't suppress the elation that bubbled within her. She did not know what the future would bring, but in this moment knew she was happy. The children, her husband, a home on this dazzling island and now some success doing the thing she loved best.

Andreas slid a frame carefully back into one of the hives and gently secured the lid. Looking up, he saw his wife walking through the long grass towards him, the poppies brushing her bare legs and a smile lit up her face as she called him.

'Andreas, come here, I have some news. Lefteri, Sofia, come up to the terrace. I have something I want to tell you!'

As her husband and the children made their way to the table in the shade of the pergola draped in early budding vine, Phoebe went inside, re-emerging with a tray laden with a carafe of wine, water, glasses and two bottles of lemonade.

Phoebe told her family the news and Andreas felt the warmth of her happiness envelop him. Somehow the insecurities he had been feeling about the virus were momentarily cast aside by the delight he saw in the face of the woman he loved.

Andreas raised his glass. '*Yamas*. Cheers. To the "Forgotten Song".'

Chapter 1

ALL LIZ WANTED to do was sleep. She had swapped her damp pillow for a spare she had found on the top shelf of the wardrobe. She had no more tears and was exhausted. But she couldn't succumb to the overwhelming tiredness she felt, her head spinning with the events which had brought her here, alone. She had lost everything she loved and had worked for.

What the hell was that noise? Why were people letting off fireworks in the middle of the night? Liz had already spent an hour trying to block out the chanting coming from loudspeakers outside the church which she now realised was right behind the room she had rented in the village. It was no good, curiosity got the better of her. Pulling on the flared jeans and a tie-dyed t-shirt which she had discarded on the floor some hours before, she slipped on her sandals and went outside.

Rounding the corner of her pension building, she stepped right into the source of the commotion. Everywhere people stood holding lighted candles; the sight would have been serenely alluring had it not been for the fire crackers which children and their fathers were throwing around with seemingly little concern for anyone's safety. Liz screamed as a cracker went off just inches from her feet, and the tears began to fall again. Never had she felt so alone. She slumped down on the wall surrounding the church and buried her head in her hands.

'Are you OK? This is your first time in Crete for Easter I think?'

Liz looked up to see a man not much older than her holding a lit candle.

'*Sygnomi*, I'm sorry if you were startled, it is a tradition here. *Christos anesti,* Christ is risen.' The man smiled and offered his free hand. 'Georgios'.

'Elizabeth, Liz.'

As the tall man bent down, his long black hair swept across his handsome face. He took his hand back to draw the hair behind his ear before offering it again to the distressed Englishwoman.

'Where are you staying? Are you here on your own?' Georgios took her hand and sat beside her on the wall.

'I was trying to rest and my room backs onto the churchyard. I only arrived in the village this afternoon and was tired. And yes, I am on my own.' At the thought of her predicament, Liz wiped her sleeve across her eyes as they began to well up again.

'It is past midnight and Easter Day, the happiest day of the year. You must not be alone, or so sad.'

There was an allure in the man's eyes which made Liz feel at ease. She managed a smile.

'I am going with my family now to our house in the village to drink some soup. It is the end of our fast. Please join us. *Ella*. Come.'

Something about the stranger made Liz feel safer than she had at almost any time since she had arrived on the island almost a month before. Suddenly she felt her exhaustion slip away.

'I'd like that.'

At her response, Georgios' smile opened up. As he stood, the candle he was holding flickered and he put his other hand around the flame to shield it.

Liz rose from the wall, looked down at her dirty jeans and crumpled top and ran a hand through her un-brushed long blond hair. 'Perhaps I shouldn't…' She could only imagine the state she was in.

'You look fine.' Georgios had read her thoughts.

Liz was not so sure but was reluctant to miss the moment.

'Let's go, my parents' house is only down the lane, they will be pleased to welcome you.'

Standing, Liz joined Georgios as he tagged along behind a group talking and laughing noisily. Each family member held a candle, all lit from the Holy Light that had been passed around by the priest during the service. In the narrow midnight streets, the flames reflected the stars shining above in the clearest of night skies.

A short way down the stone-paved street the party arrived at a traditional whitewashed cottage, its blue shutters open and fixed back. As each member of the group passed through the open door, they marked a cross in soot on the doorway with the lit candles. After making his mark, Georgios passed his candle to Liz.

'Go on, you do it too, it's good luck.' Taking her hand he guided it to make the mark.

Inside, Liz was introduced to the family, each member of which welcomed her, none of them seeming to question why a stranger should be amongst them. Georgios led her through the house and out of a door onto a raised terrace. Candle lanterns had been placed on the low wall which surrounded the paved space, half-shaded by a pergola. A large wooden table was already starting to fill up with glasses, jugs of wine, bottles of water, baskets of bread and bowls for soup.

Liz joined Georgios as he stood staring out over the wall.

'I never tire of this view. Although I no longer live here and whatever is happening to our country, this will always be here.'

Liz followed Georgios' eyes as he stared down the mountainside. She could pick out the silver leaves of thousands of olive trees highlighted in the moonlight. Far below, the reflections of the lights of waterfront tavernas glistened in the bay. A firework lit up the night sky, accompanied by the bark of a dog.

'This is not your home?' Liz enquired.

'It is my home, well, my family home. But I live in Rethymnon. I have come back to my village for Easter,' explained Georgios.

'Where is Rethymnon?' Liz wondered if she would be thought foolish at not knowing this after already a month on the island, but wanted to know more about the man who had befriended her.

'It's an old seaside town about one hundred and fifty kilometres to the west of here. I live in the city but help out my uncle on his farm in a nearby village, the rest of the time I study.'

'What are you studying?' she asked.

8

'Music. I take lessons on the lyra from an old master there, which is the real reason that I moved away,' Georgios answered.

'I'm a musician too. Well...' Liz hesitated. 'I play the guitar a bit and sing. What's a lyra?' Liz had never heard of the instrument.

'Maybe I will play a little later and you will see; and I would like to hear about your music. Let's get a drink. Do you like wine?' Liz nodded and Georgios turned to the table to pour a glass of white from an earthenware jug.

'*Yamas! Kalo Pascha*. Cheers! Happy Easter.' Georgios raised his glass.

'Happy Easter.' Liz lifted her drink and smiled. For the first time in ages she realised she was content.

'Will you excuse me a moment, I need to say hello to some relatives. Help yourself to drink and mezzes.' Georgios gestured to the now heavily laden table. 'I'll be back in a bit.'

Turning to the view down the mountain she let the friendly chatter wash over her, relishing the equanimity she felt. How long was it since she had been so at peace with the world? Thinking back, a cloud began to pass over her thoughts. She always returned to this point. Not much more than a year ago she had the world at her feet. That's what her parents had told her that day. That day when she had both been offered a job singing backing vocals on the

UK tour of an emerging folk artist and had won a place studying music at university.

The tour would run throughout the summer, including the smaller stages at some of the larger festivals, and end in September, just before the university year began. The tour had gone well, she had learned a lot and made friends and had gained confidence to dive into university life. She had loved freshers' week and settled in to her halls of residence, made more friends and thrown herself into her studies and social life in equal measure. She relished the freedom that the early Seventies and leaving home offered her and could not, she thought, have been happier.

Not much more than a month after starting her course she had got a phone call from her mother. Her mum and dad were splitting up. Apparently what Liz had always thought of as the solid foundation of her family had been unable to sustain her leaving home. Her happiness turned to grief at the loss of her family life, then anger, then to guilt. She started missing lectures and seminars, spending too much time in the student union bar.

Liz forced herself to turn away from the view down the mountainside to shake herself from the path those memories were taking her down. She could see Georgios on the other side of the terrace talking animatedly to a group of people. For a moment he turned and caught her eye. In an instant he crossed the terrace and returned to her side.

'I am sorry. It was selfish of me to leave you alone in a house full of strangers,' he apologised. 'Let's go and join the others.'

Georgios shepherded Liz around the assembled family and friends who made her feel welcome. Some spoke to her in English before reverting to Greek but even though she could not understand what was being said, Liz felt the warmth of their conversation. Occasionally Georgios would translate a sentence or a word but to Liz it hardly mattered, all she knew was that she was happy.

Excusing herself she left the group, stepping down off the terrace into the adjoining grove of olive trees. She looked up through the branches at the sky above and breathed in the scent of the mountain herbs. The air was still warm and as she walked she felt the graze of the blooms of wild flowers against her legs. She had been on the island for almost a month, why had she never felt this way before? For most of her time here she had hated it, but when had she really stopped to take in all that was around her?

She walked downhill, away from the gossip on the terrace, wanting to savour the change the night's events had made to her mood. She glanced at her watch; it was half past one. It was little more than a day since she had walked away from Bob, leaving him

11

drunk amongst the litter of bodies and rubbish that lay on the beach at Vai far to the east.

*

Bob had not come after her as she carried her rucksack and guitar to the road through the date palms. She was exhausted but too upset to sleep and just kept walking. Not long after first light she had managed to hitch a lift into the town of Sitia before buying a bus ticket to Agios Nikolaos. She didn't know where she was going, but knew she needed to get away from the life that she was leading.

Fitfully sleeping on the rattletrap bus, her dreams and waking moments alike had filled her with an anxiety too trenchant to be quelled by the spectacular vistas glimpsed through the windows. Arriving exhausted in the gleaming seaside town, she had found a waterside taverna were she could both satisfy the hunger in her stomach and take stock of her situation.

Staring out onto the bay of Mirabello, she had felt her eyes open to the beauty that surrounded her. For weeks she had been exhausted as she tagged along with Bob's dream of living in the caves at Matala then on the beach at Vai. He had then planned for them to follow the hippy trail through Turkey to India. Why had she left England with a man she had only just met at university, allowing him to persuade her to drop out and go away with him?

Yes, she had fancied him and had fallen easily into his arms in the aftermath of the devastating news of her parents' separation.

She had also been flattered when he praised her musicianship and was seduced by tales of following in the footsteps of Joni Mitchell, who had visited Matala just a few years before and celebrated the island in her hit song *Carey*. Bob had told Liz that she would develop more as a musician being out in the real world rather than studying at a stuffy university. But really it had only been his own dream that he was interested in. That dream had soon become a nightmare for Liz. Even before they had been driven out of the cave commune by the police of Greece's ruling military Junta, she had begun to hate the dirt and indolence of a life Bob seemed to revel in. He was content to spend every day drinking and smoking on the beach. Occasionally he would ask Liz to play guitar for the benefit of his friends, whilst he basked in her reflected glory.

Liz had been scared when the police had come and cleared the commune from the caves. Bob had reassured her that the palm beach at Vai would be a safe place for them to stay until they decided to take up the trail again to India. But the picture her boyfriend had painted of this idyllic beach at the far north eastern corner of Crete was just an illusion.

At one time Vai must have been stunning, but this piece of paradise had been destroyed by the cigarette butts, bottles, cans and other detritus discarded by the inhabitants of the shanty town of tents and makeshift shelters pitched by the beach.

Bob had instantly reverted to the ways of Matala; he loved the lazy lifestyle and didn't appear to mind the squalour as long as he could get drugs to smoke and alcohol to drink. As the days went by, Liz's bored mind wandered to what she had left behind, memories of her childhood and the dreams she had of becoming a performer. The futility of her present existence stood in stark contrast to the way she had felt standing on stage at a music festival or playing her guitar for an audience in the pubs and clubs back home.

Now she was alone. She sat back in the taverna chair, closed her eyes and allowed the warm rays of the sun to soothe her.

'Can I get you a drink?' A waiter woke Liz from her trance.

'I'm sorry, I was nodding off. Yes, I would love an orange juice. And can I see a menu please?'

She settled for chicken and potatoes roasted in lemon juice and olive oil served with salad and when the waiter brought her some fruit to follow she was not sure she could eat any more.

'Where are you travelling to?' Putting down a small glass and pouring her a measure of raki, he asked the question to which Liz had no idea of the answer. She downed the drink in one.

'I don't really know. I suppose I need to find a room and then plan what I am going to do. Do you know of anywhere I can stay?'

The waiter was quick to answer. 'Yes of course. It is not too far but my aunt has rooms to rent in a small village near Elounda. You go by bus to Elounda and walk up the mountain. Tell her Theo sent you.'

Theo wrote his aunt's name on a piece of paper from his pad. 'When you get to the village show anyone this and they will direct you to the place. It's easy.'

Arriving in the pretty seaside town of Elounda, she had been directed up the road to the village of Pano Elounda. Walking up the mountain road, Liz was sure that her idea of 'not too far' was wildly different from Theo's. The sense of wellbeing she had felt sitting in his taverna by the sea had been replaced by exhaustion and a fear of the unknown. It may only have been about a kilometre away, but up the steep hill in the searing afternoon sun, to an exhausted Liz it seemed to take an eternity.

Theo had been right, though, and with relief Liz was pointed in the direction of his aunt's house. She was shown into a simple room with a bed, wardrobe, table and chair and a small balcony. Putting her rucksack and guitar case on the floor she fell on the bed and for some hours tossed and turned, desperate to get to sleep but unable to free her mind enough to succumb. At some stage she must have

15

discarded her jeans and top and got under the single cotton sheet but the sleep she so desperately needed was elusive.

*

Walking through the olive grove behind the village house she could hear the lively chitchat of the guests on the terrace. Although tired, Liz no longer felt the need for sleep. The place where anxiety had throbbed in her head had been replaced by a feeling of contentment.

A mysterious noise punctured the night air; long, drawn out and musical to its core. What was that? Turning she thought she caught sight of something. She stared into the darkness. Was someone hiding, had she imagined a man in a long coat dart behind a tree? No, nothing, it must have been the haunting music making her see things. Now the mystical sound drew her back to the light of the terrace.

The music was like nothing Liz had ever heard before. The notes hung in the trees and bounced off the hills before inhabiting every part of her body. Now she could see Georgios sitting, a strange instrument perched upright on his knee as he drew the bow across its three strings. It made a sound that, although unfamiliar to Liz, seemed deeply rooted in that spot and that moment. It was as if the surrounding landscape had at that moment given birth to the music.

For the first time since she had met them the guests had fallen silent, entranced by Georgios' playing. Then he began to sing, his voice mirroring the aching notes before dropping into and weaving its way around the interstices of the melody. Liz was captivated, and something inside told her that it would change her life forever. Reaching the terrace, she sat on the wall as Georgios started another song. This time the guests joined in, punching their fists in the air. A loud bang made her jump. Another fire cracker? Looking around, she saw a young man holding a smoking gun above his head before shooting again into the air.

As the sound of gunfire echoed round the mountains the guests repeated a word from the chorus of the song.

'"*Eleftheria!*" It means "freedom".' A young woman of about Liz's own age held out a plate. 'Would you like an egg?

I am Anna. Georgios' sister,' said the pretty, petite woman with a welcoming smile.

'Liz.' Holding out her hand, she stared at the red eggs in front of her.

'Here take one, when my brother stops his music we will play a game with them. It's a tradition. Have you had soup?'

Liz watched as the friendly dark-haired woman went to the table and returned with a bowl.

17

'It is made from the lamb we are roasting for tomorrow's lunch.' She turned and nodded in the direction of the corner of the terrace, where several elderly men were busying themselves around the carcass of a whole lamb on a spit mounted over a large barbecue. 'Has my brother invited you to lunch? Sometimes he can forget his manners. You must come.'

As Liz took a spoonful she struggled to disguise a grimace at the pungent flavour. Anna caught her expression. 'It's an acquired taste. The roast lamb will be better I can assure you,' said Anna, smiling.

'I'd love to come to lunch, as long as I can get some sleep first! Why was that man shooting a gun?' Liz decided to broach the thing that was worrying her.

'For some people it is a tradition at celebrations, weddings and at Easter. But in these times it also shows that we will never be defeated. It is a symbol of our freedom, of how we will not be enslaved by the fascist dictatorship of the Colonels. Georgios was singing a traditional song of freedom. The Junta does not allow them to be sung, but we have endured rule by the Turks, invasion by the Germans, a civil war, we are not afraid of those tin pot soldiers.'

When she had come to Crete, Liz had known nothing of its history. She had heard snippets about the ruling authoritarian regime when the police had harried the commune away from the caves at Matala. She wanted to learn more about what was going on in the country, but now was not the time. Georgios had changed the mood of the gathering in an instant as he increased the tempo of the music, winding it up as his bow bounced across the strings. One by one the guests stood and joined a line of dancers making a circle among the olive trees.

'*Ella*. Here, come and dance.' Anna pulled Liz towards the steps. Leaving her egg on the wall she allowed herself to be led from the terrace to the olive grove.

'I can't,' she protested, laughing, as she was cajoled into the line of dancers.

Linking her arm around Anna's shoulders, Liz looked down at her feet and tried to follow the steps. At the other end of the line a man held up a red scarf in his free hand and was leaping acrobatically, slapping the heel of his boot as he appeared to float in the air. Liz was growing more confident and stopped looking at her feet, letting the rhythm of the music take her. She watched the lead dancer jump higher as Georgios played faster and faster. On the terrace the other guests clapped and shouts of '*Opa!*' rang out accompanied by a salvo of gunshots. The music built and built towards a crescendo then suddenly stopped.

'Bravo!' Anna congratulated Liz, who was trying to get her breath back. 'Let's go and find a drink.'

'I see you've met my little sister?' Georgios approached carrying his lyra and glistening with sweat. 'Did you like the music?'

'I loved it. I have never heard anything like it before.' Liz could hear herself gushing.

'You must play your guitar for me some day. You say you are a musician?'

'Was.' Liz heard herself say.

'If you are a musician, you are a musician. You can never lose it. It is part of your soul.' As Georgios spoke, Liz could feel the blood rising in her cheeks. She knew in her heart what he said was true and was embarrassed about how she had betrayed herself by running away from the thing she loved best.

Seeing Liz's discomfort, Anna quickly changed the subject. 'I have invited Liz to lunch.'

'Of course you must come. I can borrow a guitar, maybe you can play?'

'I have mine with me back in the room.' Liz spoke before she realised that she was agreeing to play. 'I don't know. I'm very tired. I haven't played in public for ages...' She was running out of excuses.

'Tomorrow is another day. Well it's not, actually.' Georgios looked at his watch. 'Lunch is later today,' he said and laughed.

'I really should go and get some sleep,' Liz stood to leave.

'Here, we must do the eggs before you go.' Anna reached for her egg, picked up one for her brother as Liz retrieved hers from where she had left it on the wall.

Anna and Georgios were like children as they showed Liz how to knock the hard red eggs against each others', explaining that the person whose egg cracked last would have good luck for the following year.

Georgios' cracked first, followed by his sister's.

'Beginner's luck!' Anna cried, but Liz was not sure that her hosts had not let her win.

'You are the lucky one.' Georgios' eyes sparkled as he congratulated Liz.

'I really must go. Thank you for a lovely evening.'

'*Parakalo*. You are welcome. We will see you for lunch.' Georgios led his guest to the front door. 'Can I show you home?'

'I'll be fine,' Liz said. 'I'll see you in a few hours.'

'Bring your guitar.' Georgios shouted after her as she walked up the lane.

A gentle breeze brushed her cheek and an early cockerel crowed, a reminder of the lateness of the hour. Turning to look down the hillside, Liz saw the lights of a fishing boat making its way into the tiny harbour of Elounda. The kindness, hospitality and friendship she had discovered that night had worked its alchemy and the music of the lyra had rekindled something in her soul. It had made her aware of what in recent months she had forgotten; that for her, music was elemental to her being. Maybe she would take her guitar to the lunch tomorrow.

Collapsing on her bed, she fell into a deep sleep, the beguiling melody of a lyra playing through her dreams. Perhaps she had turned a corner and the scarlet egg would bring her luck?

Chapter 2

AS THE LIGHT crept around the shutters in her room, Liz threw open the windows. Despite having only slept for a few hours she felt refreshed and wide awake. Picking up her watch from the chair beside the bed, she saw it was only just after 9 o'clock. She had four hours to wait before she saw Georgios again.

It took her some time to wash in the lukewarm trickle of water in the shower, and to brush the knots out of her hair. She found a clean but crumpled cotton dress at the bottom of her rucksack. Putting it on, she smoothed it with her hands, hoping the worst of the creases would fall out with wear. By the time she had made herself presentable it was still not 11 o'clock. She was dying for a coffee.

Letting herself out of the door, the warmth of the spring sunshine hit her. She blinked as her eyes adjusted to the sunlight then came to focus on the array of geraniums of all colours growing out of cracks in the path and purple bougainvillea hanging from the wall of her building. Everything about the new day was calling her outside. Liz stepped down into the alley and set out to find a shop. She soon realised that this was unlikely in the sleepy village where only the night before firecrackers had pierced the air. She was just debating whether to walk down to the waterfront at Elounda when she noticed a small, grey-haired woman, wearing an apron, waving to her.

'*Ella*, come,' the woman called from where she sat at a small iron table outside a building which to Liz was not discernibly different to the other houses.

As she got closer, through the windows of the building Liz saw it was a kafenio. The owner gestured for her to take a seat, and Liz managed to communicate that she would like coffee. She watched as the woman went inside, putting coffee, water and sugar into the long-handled briki before placing it on what looked like a camping stove. Stirring the coffee, her host watched it intently until just as it began to bubble, she took it off the heat and poured it into a small cup. Filling a glass with water from the tap over the sink she took a biscuit from an open packet and put it on a plate, bringing them outside to Liz.

The coffee was strong and sweet and Liz was grateful for the water. The owner pulled a chair up to the table and the two sat there happy, occasionally trying to communicate through gestures. When Liz reached into her bag for her purse the woman put a hand to her heart. The coffee was an act of hospitality. Touched by the generosity, Liz gave the woman a hug before turning back down the alley to her room.

It was still only midday. Liz was itching to see her new friends again. 'Bring your guitar' were the last words Georgios had shouted after her as she left the house in the early hours. She picked the case up from the floor and put it on the bed. It was filthy. She had carted it with her as she traipsed around the island with Bob, but only rarely had the guitar come out of its case. Taking a flannel from her wash bag, she wiped the grime off the black leather. Beneath the dirt were stickers reminding her of gigs she had played, places she had been, small triumphs in what had been a burgeoning music career.

As she cleaned away the muck of her ill-advised adventure with Bob and the case began to shine, her spirit began to lift. Why had she left the instrument in its case for all this time? For much of her life she had lived for singing, writing songs and playing the guitar. She flicked the catches on the case and lifted the lid. Inside was the instrument given to her by her mum and dad when she had got her first paid gig. A tear came to her eye as she thought about her parents and their separation and how they had invested so much, maybe too much, of their lives into her future. Had her leaving home to go to university left such a hole in their relationship that their marriage had imploded into the void?

She was pleased to see that not a speck of dust had got inside the case, and she took the guitar by the neck and gently removed it and put the strap over her shoulder. She opened a compartment in the case, taking out her capo and clipping it to the head before reaching down for a plectrum. Tuning the instrument by ear she reached for her pipes to check she had not lost her perfect pitch. Tentatively she strummed the strings, as her left hand began moving around the fretboard with a certainty that surprised even herself.

After just a few moments she managed to rekindle the joy that playing the instrument gave her. Quietly at first she began to sing to herself before letting her voice get louder and her ears rather than her head hear the sound. She smiled when she realised she was still in tune and became more adventurous, rediscovering the range that her voice could travel. As she grew in confidence she let the music take her wherever it would. Glancing at her watch she noticed it was already ten past one. Replacing her guitar in its red velvet bed she snapped the case shut.

The door to Georgios' parent's house was open. Liz hovered on the step before someone she didn't recognise ushered her inside the crowded room. Looking around she spotted Anna.

'I'm sorry I'm late!'

'Are you?' Anna shrugged. 'We are here all day. Come onto the terrace. Georgios is outside with the men tending the barbecue.'

Squeezing past the guests inside the house, they emerged back into the sunlight, where the delicious smell of roasting lamb and herbs hit Liz and she was led to the table and poured a glass of wine by Anna. In the corner of the terrace an elderly man turned a spit over the coals whilst holding an animated conversation with Georgios who was basting the lamb with a bunch of twigs. The fat made a spitting noise as it hit the red-hot coals and, taking a knife, Georgios carved a slice of meat and put it in his mouth. Looking up, he saw his sister with Liz watching him and cut another slice.

'Here, try some. It tastes great.' Georgios held out his knife to Liz.

Putting her guitar case down, she took the meat from the blade. She had never tasted lamb like it. Anna handed her a paper napkin from the table.

'It's delicious,' Liz said, wiping fat from her chin.

'I'm pleased you came.' Georgios said, kissing her on both cheeks. 'I see you brought your guitar.'

Liz felt her face redden at the thought of playing in front of this man who she hardly knew. She had played in front of audiences many a time, so why did she feel so different about playing to this enigmatic stranger?

'You can play for us later maybe?' Liz felt a flutter of excitement at the thought.

'Would you like to try the *kokoretsi*?' Georgios pointed to long skewers cooking over one end of the grill.

'What is it?' Liz asked.

'It is not to everyone's taste.' Anna advised. 'It is the offal of the lamb, wrapped in its intestines and caul fat.'

'It's delicious.' Georgios cut through a piece and slid it off the skewer, offering it to Liz on his knife.

'I'll leave it for the time being, if it's all the same to you.'

Smiling, he held her glance for a moment as he put the knife to his own mouth. 'Maybe you would like to try some later?'

The smell of lemon, thyme and oregano was making Liz hungry.

'Why don't you sit down at the table and I will come and join you when I have helped my father carve the meat?'

Leaving a space for Georgios, Anna and Liz sat down at the long terrace table which had been laid with salads, bread and jugs of wine. As his father carved meat onto trays, Georgios brought plates laden with roasted potatoes and the platters of lamb and *kokoretsi* from the grill.

There must have been twenty guests seated at the long table and it seemed to Liz that they were all talking at once and she could understand little of what was being said. But one thing was certain, the food was delicious. In the warmth of the sun she let the babble of the guests sink into the background as she stared at the view that the previous night had been shrouded in darkness. In the distance she could see a large island that looked as though it was attached to the mainland by a bridge over a small canal leading to an expanse of sparkling blue water flanked by spectacular mountains. On the near side of the canal, boats criss-crossed the bay leaving fine traces of white thread across its iridescent waters.

'They will be heading to Spinalonga.' Liz was jolted from her musing by Georgios sitting down beside her. 'The boats. It's a holiday, so many people will go to visit the island. You cannot quite see it from here, but just off the other end of that island attached to the causeway is the leper island.'

Liz sat entranced as Georgios related the story of how Spinalonga had once been a Venetian fortress, and had in more

29

recent times become a leper colony, its last residents leaving as recently as 17 years earlier in 1957. She was amazed to consider that there had been patients living there in the years after her birth.

As soon as Liz's plate was empty, either Anna or Georgios would serve her more. Not wanting to be rude, Liz ate until she felt she could not swallow another mouthful. With the plates cleared from the first course, the table was replenished with trays of honeyed pastries and bowls of fruit along with more wine and carafes of raki. Liz found herself opening up to her new friends about how she had come to be on the island and the circumstances which had led her to the village the day before. The sun was already turning orange and was beginning to sink behind the surrounding mountains. Liz knew she had had more to drink than she was used to but somehow didn't feel drunk, just imbued with warmth inside at a perfect afternoon.

Guests at the other end of the table were calling Georgios' name, then chanting it and clapping. Excusing himself he went inside and returned with his music case.

'They want him to play.' Anna said and Liz could see the pride for her brother in the young woman's sparkling, deep brown eyes.

Immediately Georgios drew his bow across the strings, Liz was reminded of the moment the night before when she had first heard him play. Looking across to where he now sat on the terrace wall with the olive grove behind him, the lyra resting on his knee, when he flicked back his long black hair she could see in his face his utter immersion in the music. He was at one with the instrument as the music rose and fell away as though it was part of the mountains and the valleys that surrounded them. Looking up she could see the faint crescent of the moon sharing the sky with the fading sun. An eagle flew high above her, silhouetted against the last vestiges of the daylight. Cries of '*Opa!*' and 'Bravo!' rang out from around the table as Georgios warmed to his task, drawing the guests in to his mystical musical world.

Just like the night before, it was no time before the guests were dancing down in the olive grove, and it took little encouragement from Anna to persuade Liz to join in. The line wove its way through the trees, a different dancer taking the lead with each song, their acrobatic leaps getting more adventurous.

After three dances, exhausted, Liz dropped out of the line.

'I need to take a breather,' she told Anna, her friend joining her as she strolled further into the olive grove.

'You're a good dancer,' said Anna, 'you learned quickly.'

'I think you are just being kind,' laughed Liz, enjoying the flattery. Suddenly she stopped.

'What was that? I'm sure I saw somebody watching us from behind a tree down there. I thought I saw someone last night too.'

31

'Let's take a look,' said Anna.

Liz was not sure of the wisdom of investigating further but Anna strode towards the trees she had indicated. As they approached, a shady figure in a long coat ran out from his hiding place and headed further into the olive grove.

'Are you not a bit warm in that coat, Stelio?' Anna shouted.

Stopping in his tracks, a young man turned to face them.

'This has got to stop! I have told you so many times that I am not interested. Now go before I call my brother.'

A mixture of fear and humiliation crossed the man's face before he turned and walked quickly down the hillside.

'This is the last time, Stelio, stop pestering me,' Anna called after him.

'I'm sorry if he scared you,' Anna said to Liz. 'We went to school together and he has got it into his head that I might want to go out with him. He used to be pathetic, but now he has found himself some new friends, some are saying he is a spy for the Junta.'

'Does that not worry you?' Liz asked.

'Look at him in that ridiculous coat, skulking about hiding behind trees, he does not scare me. Promise me one thing though, Liz, don't tell Georgios about him. He might take it a bit more seriously than I do and then heaven knows where it might end. Let's go back and join the others.'

The dancers had left the olive grove and the up-tempo music had been replaced with a more plaintive, melancholic melody. The lyra was now joined by another instrument.

'That is heavenly,' commented Liz.

'My father is playing the bouzouki alongside Georgios. He likes to play *rebetika*.'

'What is rebetika?' Liz asked.

'It is not like anything else really, perhaps it has some of the sentiment of blues,' explained Anna. 'It is soulful and individualistic, usually sad, and the songs are about the Greek spirit and our past. Many, like this one, are about freedom and often have been banned by our leaders who fear them as being subversive. The Junta hate it and many musicians have been imprisoned, tortured or worse just for playing it. But they will never stop.'

When they reached the terrace, Liz noticed that the guests were listening in silence and she watched as one man danced alone, entranced. When the music came to an end the only applause was the hush of reverence.

Seeing the two women, Georgios put down his lyra.

'Will you play for us now?' he asked Liz.

Any confidence she may have felt earlier evaporated. How could she compete with the powerful songs she had just heard?

'Come on, you are among friends, there is nothing to be scared of,' encouraged Georgios.

Of course he was right. Liz recalled what Georgios had said the night before, that if you are a musician then music is part of your soul. Hadn't she played before audiences much bigger than this?

Taking her guitar from the case, she let herself be led to the place on the wall where Georgios had been performing. She took a plectrum from her pocket and put it in her mouth, running her fingers across the strings and adjusting the tune. Then, taking the plectrum, she drew it across the strings. Even at that moment she didn't know what she was going to play. She heard her own voice, clear and smooth, and her instincts kicked in and she found herself playing a set she had performed so often in pubs and music clubs back home. The guests fell silent, enraptured by her mellow voice and the lightness of her touch. Now, as she worked through her repertoire of covers of Dylan, Cat Stevens and Joni Mitchell mixed with her own compositions, any nerves she had felt disappeared.

She could tell from the applause that her music was appreciated. She was enjoying herself but was concerned that she might be going on too long so brought her performance to a close.

As she walked back towards where Georgios was sitting with his sister the guests stood, some patting her on the back as she passed.

'Bravo!' Georgios stood clapping. 'That wasn't so bad, was it?'

'You were wonderful,' Anna chipped in.

Liz felt the warmth of being appreciated which she had not experienced for some time. This was how she used to feel when she finished a performance. How had she let the events of the past few months wipe that from her memory?

'Thank you. And thank you, Georgios, for persuading me to play. I had forgotten how good it makes me feel.'

'I'm pleased I did, you must never stop singing and playing. And your own songs are incredible; authentic and straight from the heart.' Georgios got up and went to the table returning with three tumblers of wine.

'Here's to the future.' As the three of them drank a toast, Liz considered how in a day her world had been turned around.

Casual in each other's company, they talked about music and in Georgios Liz saw a reflection of herself, in the passion he shared for playing. How unlike Bob he was, she thought. When Georgios talked his eyes lit up and when they met hers, he held her in his gaze. How different to the empty stare of the man who she had followed out to this island. Although she had only known Georgios and Anna for a day, Liz felt herself opening up about the breakdown of her parents' marriage and how she had left university and run away with Bob to Crete. Brother and sister were good listeners and Liz felt liberated as she unburdened herself of the recent past.

'One thing you must never do is to stop playing your music,' Georgios insisted. 'It is a gift that you have been given and must never be taken for granted. Even in the worst of times it will see you through.'

Her performance that evening had proved Georgios right. It had been a long time since Liz had felt so at ease. Strange, she reflected, how being with people she had just met in a place she had just arrived in could make her feel so carefree.

'What do you think?' Georgios' voice penetrated her thoughts.

'I'm sorry, I was miles away.' Liz was brought back to the present by the deep brown eyes of the handsome man staring at her.

'Spinalonga, would you like to come with me tomorrow? I have to travel back to Rethymnon the next day so it will be my last chance to show you the island.'

Liz's heart leaped at the thought of spending time with Georgios then dived again when she realised he was leaving the following day.

'Yes, I would love that, it sounds interesting.' Liz instantly decided she would rather spend one day with Georgios than face the prospect of never seeing him again.

'Unfortunately, I have things to do, so won't be joining you,' said Anna, not entirely convincingly.

'Then it looks like it will be just the two of us, if you don't mind that?' Georgios raised an eyebrow.

'No, no. Not at all.' Liz couldn't think of anything at that moment that she would have minded less.

*

The following morning, Liz slipped the bolts on the shutters and threw them open to welcome in the early sunshine. Anticipation had awoken her from her slumbers and she had struggled to get back to sleep as she thought about the day ahead. But what would she do after that? When she had left Bob on the beach at Vai she had made no plans other than to get as far away from him as she could. Maybe she would go home; she had a standby ticket from Athens to Heathrow in her rucksack. But that was before she had come to the village and met Georgios. Now she wanted more than anything to stay, but if Georgios was leaving, would she feel the same?

She tossed and turned but could not find an answer. She decided to enjoy the day and see where events led her. After all, it was serendipity that had brought her here in the first place. She was soon showered and dressed, went to the kafenio and drank two coffees and it was still an hour before Georgios had arranged to call for her. She sat on the wooden chair on the small balcony and looked down towards Elounda and the bay stretching away to the canal and beyond that to the mountains. She pondered on the luck that had brought her to this little piece of paradise.

As she surveyed the olive groves, for the first time since the previous summer she felt a tune come into her head. Wordless, the chords danced there, inviting a melody to bring them to life. Liz reached for her guitar. The song came easily, and Liz jotted it down on a stave hastily drawn on a scrap piece of paper lest the music should escape her. Looking down the lane, she saw Georgios climbing the hill to her pension and stuffing the paper in the case alongside her guitar she went to the door.

They walked downhill through the lanes, where the only traffic was a vendor selling fruit and vegetables from the back of his pick-up truck. Liz wondered how he managed to navigate it through the narrow streets, though the dents and scrapes on its battered bodywork suggested sometimes he was unable to thread his vehicle through the eye of a needle.

A group of elderly women dressed in their widows' weeds wished them '*kalimera*, good morning' as they sat taking in the morning sunshine. The old donkey track out of the village passed under the road that Liz remembered struggling up to get to the village not two days before. Then she had been tired and could think of little else but to find a room for the night. Today, going down the mountainside, the view opened up the whole wealth of possibilities which the day had to offer.

She could feel the heat of the rough cobbles under the thin soles of her shoes as the sun rose higher in the sky. A dog barked, rushing to the end of its leash, scaring Liz, but Georgios rubbed its head whispering '*katse kala*' and it sat, its tail brushing the dusty earth. Ahead, down the hillside, the bay glistened enticingly. Unable to take her eyes off the ultramarine waters, Liz stumbled on the uneven stones and Georgios reached out and caught her hand.

'I know it is difficult but you must look down, we will be on the water soon enough.' Georgios pressed her hand before slowly letting go.

Passing through the back streets of the seaside town, Georgios took pride in explaining that the square and little harbour to which they were heading had only been completed two years before. As they emerged onto the quayside, Liz could see why he was so proud. Where before fishermen had pulled their boats up onto the beach, now their caiques sat moored to a quayside alongside the *plateia* bordered by shops and tavernas and the dazzling white of the new church and its belfry framed by palm trees.

Stopping at a *periptero*, Georgios bought some drinks from the kiosk before heading for the waterfront. Fishermen were selling the last of their night's catch and mending nets on the quayside. Cats languished in the sun, keeping one eye open for the spoils left behind when the trading finished. Georgios greeted one of the fishermen, then stepped down onto a small caique, holding out his arm for Liz to follow him aboard.

'He is my friend and is lending us his boat to go to Spinalonga. As long as we get it back here for him to work tonight, it will be fine.'

Going astern, Georgios walked around the small cabin and dropped down into the cockpit, checked the gear lever for neutral and turned over the engine. Walking forward again, he led Liz by the hand into the cockpit before returning and slipping the mooring at the bow and joining her aft, leaning over the stern to pull the boat back and untie it from the floating mooring buoy. Adrift, he eased the lever into reverse and grabbed the tiller, gently steering the vessel away from the quayside.

The caique smelled of fish and salt, but even the smoke from the noisy engine could not take away from the joy Liz felt at being on the water. A trail of bubbles followed them, and as they passed out of the harbour walls Georgios pointed, saying, 'Spinalonga'. In the distance she could see a small island offshore of another larger island linked by a bridge to the causeway, which she had seen from the terrace up in the village.

The rounded walls and ramparts of a fortress became clearer as they approached. Georgios throttled back the engine so he could make himself heard, explaining how the defences on Spinalonga had been built by the Venetians during their occupation and had been the last stronghold of their rule on the island. They held out there against the Ottoman invaders for nearly half a century after the rest of Crete had fallen.

When Crete was finally declared an independent state in 1898 the Ottoman troops who had used Spinalonga as a fortress left, leaving a small civilian population of Turkish Cretans who remained until the fledgling state designated it a leper colony in 1904. From the calm waters of the bay of Korfos, to Liz the island looked idyllic and she found it difficult to imagine the suffering which had inhabited that place until only 17 years ago.

Georgios stood at the helm watching his course. As they approached, the forbidding stone walls which rose around the island came into stark focus. Navigating the boat alongside a crumbling quay, Georgios looped a rope through a mooring ring set in the stones. Cutting the engine he jumped ashore, holding out a hand to help Liz onto the jetty.

The entrance to the village where the patients had lived was called Dante's Gate. Liz shuddered to think how many of the people passing through here knew that they would never return. Some patients who were sent to the island were later found to be healthy, and a few escaped by swimming to the mainland but for most it was the place where they would live out their lives.

Liz had not known what she had expected but, although dilapidated, the village was not unlike so many others she had seen dotted around Crete. There were the remains of shops, tavernas, and a hospital where the sickest patients had been treated. Georgios explained that, since the residents had left, the village had been plundered for building materials which had been shipped across the strait to Elounda, Plaka and further afield. He told her he hoped some day that the spot would be restored as a fitting tribute to those who had died and a place where perhaps foreign tourists would visit.

Flowers bloomed through the tumbling walls and a cat sat on the step of the locked church of Agios Panteleimonas, the patron saint of lepers. Georgios pointed to an inscription commemorating how the church was restored by the island residents in 1953. Despite the seeming normality of the ramshackle village, for Liz it was difficult to shake off the lingering reminder of what life must have been like for those forced to spend their days here.

'When my parents were younger, they remember the boatman rowing patients and supplies across to the island from Plaka,' Georgios said. 'There are still people alive who were once patients here.'

She was pleased when they left the village behind, following the path around the island to its northern tip, where a crescent-shaped fortress stood guard over the straits leading into the bay. Liz found it hard to reconcile such beauty with the eerie sense she got of the island's history. The story of Spinalonga was almost overwhelming in its anguish.

Staring across the bay, Liz could not stop a tear running down her cheek.

'I'm sorry, I should not have brought you. Maybe it is too upsetting?' Concerned, Georgios wrapped a comforting arm around her shoulder.

'No, no. I am pleased I came. It's unlike anywhere I have been in my life.' Liz leant into his chest, his closeness healing any disquiet she might have felt. 'I was just trying to imagine how awful it would be having your freedom taken away, however splendid your prison.'

'For some people, that was their home village.' Georgios pointed to a cluster of buildings across the water. 'Plaka, where they had families; wives, husbands, even children. It is hard to imagine what they must have felt being so close yet not being able to see their loved ones.'

Taking Liz by the hand, Georgios led her further along the path to the seaward side of the island to where a small overgrown cemetery indicated the last resting place for many of those who had lived there. The sea ran all the way to the horizon where almost imperceptibly it segued into the sky. Liz was unsure what she felt as her emotions swung between the elation of being alone with Georgios and the melancholy she sensed at the legacy of the fascinating island.

At that moment Georgios took her head in his hands and kissed her.

Chapter 3

AS GEORGIOS NAVIGATED the boat away from the island, Liz found her mind already in turmoil over the desolation of Spinalonga and the joy she felt at the kiss, brought into perspective by remembering that Georgios was leaving the following day.

She leaned forward and brushed her long blond hair behind her ear to hear what Georgios was saying over the thumping of the engine.

'Would you like to visit Plaka for lunch?' he shouted.

Smiling, she mouthed her assent.

She did not know where life was heading, but as she looked at the confident young man at the helm, she knew she had never felt anything like this before. Bob had been her first real boyfriend, and she had realised some time ago that her relationship with him was purely an escape from the pain and guilt she felt at her parents' separation. Whatever the future might bring, at the moment she knew one thing, she wanted to spend as much time as she could with Georgios.

Ahead of them, Liz could see a cluster of stone-build buildings hugging the coastline. This must be the village of Plaka which Georgios had mentioned. A quay fashioned out of huge stones jutted out into the sea, and as they approached Liz could not help thinking that this must have been the spot from where patients had left to face their uncertain future on Spinalonga.

At a taverna right on the waterfront, a waiter showed them to a table above the jetty where they had secured the caique. He wedged a pebble from the beach under a table leg to stop it from wobbling and took their order for drinks.

Condensation dripped down the glasses of beer brought by the waiter who placed a menu on the table. Picking it up, Liz realised it was no use looking at what was on offer as it was in Greek.

'Do you like fish?' Georgios asked.

'I love fish.' Liz suddenly felt ravenous at the prospect.

'Then I will order for both of us and we can share.'

Georgios shouted to the waiter who invited him into his kitchen. 'Don't worry, you will like it,' he said, leaving Liz alone at the table. The beer was cold and she could taste a salty edge. She did not know whether it was the drink or sea spray on her lips. She reached in a pocket and pulled out an elastic band, with the other hand clinching her hair into a bunch she pulled it through the loop, twisting until it held. Leaning back in the chair she allowed herself to close her eyes, the warmth of the sun momentarily brushing away any thoughts as it caressed her face.

'You are tired?' Liz started at Georgios voice.

'No, I'm just wondering if a day could be more perfect.' Liz opened her eyes and thought she might know the answer to her own question.

The conversation moved on to music, and Liz modestly told an impressed Georgios about the concerts she had played the previous summer, and he in turn explained the deep-rooted tradition of the lyra on Crete and the music he so loved performing.

There was hardly space on the table for the plate of fish: sardines striped from the grill, giant prawns with garlic, rings of fried calamari and sea bream glistening in oil and lemon sauce.

'When are you thinking of returning to England?'

Georgios' question brought Liz's mind to focus sharply on something she had been avoiding thinking about. She was falling for this man who had come into her life, and had pushed thoughts of leaving Crete to the back of her mind.

'I don't know,' she replied. 'I have a standby ticket from Athens so I can go whenever I want.'

'If you have no plans to leave soon, why don't you come to Rethymnon?'

She replied without hesitation. 'I'd love that.' A broad smile crossed Georgios' face and she thought it was relief.

Finishing the fish, they sat into the dwindling afternoon making plans for the following day. Georgios made the town sound so appealing but Liz was sure she would be happy whatever it was like.

'Is that the time?' Georgios looked at his watch, reaching for his wallet. 'We must get the boat back to my friend.'

Casting off, Georgios kept close inshore, steering along the coastline heading south. The afternoon sea breeze had dropped as the land cooled and the water was flat calm. Georgios' friend was waiting at the quay as they brought the caique to its berth, and taking the line he pulled it close to land so the couple could step out, before jumping aboard to ready his vessel for a night's fishing.

After thanking him the couple stepped out across the square.

'Shall we stop for a drink before we walk up the hill?'

Liz was just about to answer when he continued. 'On second thoughts, I think we'll give it a miss tonight.'

Taking her elbow, Georgios hastily turned Liz around and headed towards the lanes which led to the donkey track.

'Why the change of heart?' Liz turned her head to look back over her shoulder.

'In the taverna there were police, and at least one ESA or military policeman, the enforcers of the Junta. I'd rather not be any place where they are.'

Turning into the side streets, Georgios let go of Liz's arm and they relaxed their pace.

'That is the dark side of our country. They are the torturers and murderers who try to suppress our freedom, but they will never keep us down.' Liz sensed the anger in his voice as he spoke.

They hadn't gone far when a shout pierced the air: 'You bitch!'

Georgios let go of Liz's arm and ran towards a man in a long coat who stumbled backwards out of a doorway clutching his groin, letting go of a young woman. Hearing the footsteps he turned and fled.

'Anna!' Georgios panted. 'Are you OK?'

'He followed me, the bastard, but he won't be trying that again. I think my knee connected.' Anna's face had turned white and despite her voice remaining calm they could see fear in her eyes.

'Liz, can you look after Anna? I'm going to sort him out for good.' Georgios made to go after his sister's attacker but she put a restraining hand on his arm.

'No, don't do that, it's only that idiot Stelios who has pestered me ever since we were at school. I can handle him, but he has some powerful friends.'

'Those ones drinking in the taverna?' Georgios asked. Liz could see the anger written on Georgios' face.

'You saw them, did you? I walked past and heard them goading Stelios and he must have followed me. He pushed me into the doorway and tried to kiss me.'

'If you insist, I will leave it. But I cannot promise what will happen if I ever cross paths with that snivelling coward again. You must be careful, what were you doing down here?'

Anna was struggling to retain her composure and for a moment had to think hard to recall the answer to her brother's question. 'Mother had baked some cakes for Aunt Eleni's birthday and asked if I would take them to her. I stopped and had a chat and before I knew it, it was dark. I was going to take the road rather than the donkey track so I didn't twist an ankle in the darkness. And then that creep tried it on!'

Liz reached out and put her arm around Anna. A tear escaped down her cheek as the shock of her ordeal hit her. 'Let's get you home.'

As they walked up the mountain road, Georgios allowed himself to be persuaded by Anna not to mention a word of this to their father. If they did, he would likely seek out Stelios and exact revenge, which would only lead to the family being imprisoned or worse.

'Hopefully Stelios feels humiliated enough not to try anything like that again,' said Anna. Her brother was not so optimistic. 'Let's not let this ruin our last night together before you return to Rethymnon.' Anna tried to put a brave face on the situation, but Liz could see that she was shaken by the assault. They walked up the mountainside in silence, the attack foremost in their thoughts but all keen not to talk about what had happened.

Back at her parents' house Anna quickly made her excuses and took herself off to have a shower. By the time she joined the family on the terrace she had outwardly regained some composure. She was exhausted but did not want to be alone with her thoughts in bed. Not wanting to let her parents know that anything was amiss, she tried to immerse herself in the conversation. She was genuinely delighted at the news that Liz was going to Rethymnon with her brother the next day; she could see that the young musician made her brother happy. But part of her would have loved her new friend to remain in the village.

That evening they sat talking into the small hours until Georgios pointed out that the local bus to take them to Agios Nikolaos left the square in Elounda in little more than six hours. Liz said her farewells and wandered up the lane to pack her bag and fall into bed.

Sleep did not come easily; Liz found it hard to come to terms with her rapture at the kiss on Spinalonga with the menacing events of that evening in Elounda. She was excited about what the future might hold for her, but lurking in the background of her thoughts was the dark figure of the man in the long coat.

Eventually sleep took her and when she awoke she was pleased she had packed the night before as it was only 10 minutes before Georgios had said he would come and get her. She ran next door to pay Theo's aunt for her room and had just shouldered her rucksack and picked up her guitar case when Georgios arrived.

In the light of day Elounda exuded none of the menace of the previous night. In the square where the threatening presence of the police cars had loomed, they stood waiting for the bus to take them to Agios Nikolaos.

There at the bus station they bought tickets for Heraklion, where they would change for Rethymnon. Despite the music blaring from the speakers on the rickety old bus, the warmth and tiredness overcame Liz and she gave in to sleep, only to awake as the bus came to a halt with her head rested on Georgios' shoulder.

'Are we here?' she asked blearily.

Looking through the dusty window she saw the bus had parked in a square with a park in the centre.

'No, we have quite a way to go yet,' said Georgios. 'This is Neapoli. It used to be the capital of the region until the early part of the century.'

Looking around, Liz could see the town still retained an air of its past grandeur. Narrow cobbled lanes wound their way off a green open park and Liz saw the red domes of a grand cathedral, while flat-bed trucks laden with hay, fruit, vegetables and livestock went about their day-to-day business. The bus driver returned to his seat with a coffee and they continued on their way. Back on the main road they chugged up a spectacular gorge passing through the mountains. Liz glimpsed the four-tiered bell tower of a monastery rising above the forested slopes. As the bus descended again, the boulder strewn roadside bore evidence of recent seismic activity.

The road flattened as they reached the coastal plain, and Liz recognised the town of Malia, the place she had stayed with Bob the first night they had landed on the island. They passed by the small pension where they had rented a room. She remembered how she had opened the shutters onto a grove of orange trees. Leaning from the balcony she had picked a fruit before rushing outside and walking through the trees all the way to the sparkling sea, with the juice of the orange running down her chin. She had been cheerful, the future full of optimism.

Since then things had gone downhill and, looking back, Liz realised that had been the last time she had been happy until she had met Georgios. The initial joy she had felt that first morning on Crete had soon turned to boredom when they had arrived at Matala, then anger at being ignored and taken for granted.

Leaving Malia behind the bus rattled its way, hugging the coast, through seaside villages set between empty beaches of almost unimaginable beauty. The road cut inland, traversing the cliffs to bypass the airport before making its way through the potholed outskirts of the capital to the bus station beside the port. Reclaiming their bags, they boarded the bus for Rethymnon and settled down for the final stage of their journey.

Liz soon caught a glimpse of the old harbour, with brightly-coloured caiques bobbing at their moorings under the protective shadow of the Venetian castle. Leaving Heraklion, the bus began to climb, winding through groves of olive trees stepping down the mountainsides. Time and again the road would return to the sea and she could see the blue of the Mediterranean reaching out to infinity.

Heading inland again they passed through a forest, where on either side of the road farmers had set up stalls selling fruit. Bending to peek through the windows on the landward side of the bus, Liz could see the foothills of Mount Psiloritis rising up to the south. Villagers coaxed precariously loaded donkeys through narrow streets as the bus threaded its way between buildings, some flying an ominous black-and-red flag with the silhouette of a soldier set against a phoenix rising from the flames. Georgios explained it was the ensign of the military dictatorship, and Liz shuddered when she remembered the events of the night before.

In the heat the journey seemed never-ending. Despite the beauty of the changing landscapes Liz fell asleep again, only to wake as they reached Rethymnon. She was surprised when her watch told her it had not been five hours since they had had set off from the village. Stepping down from the bus gave little relief from the blazing sun and she was grateful for the shade of the narrow streets of the old town as they wound their way towards Georgios' apartment.

Climbing the dark stairs he let them in to the flat before opening the shutters onto a wooden balcony. Light flooded the room illuminating its simple interior: a bed, a small table and chair, a makeshift bookcase made of pieces of wood balanced on empty bottles, a brightly woven rug on the tiled floor. At the end of the room was a kitchenette, separated from the main living space by a counter and a door to a small shower room.

Georgios read Liz's thoughts. 'Don't worry, the apartment belongs to our family and we own the one next door. Here I will show you.'

Putting a key into the door next to his own, Georgios opened it onto an almost identical flat.

'Will you be OK here?' he asked.

'This is great,' she answered, a smile trying to hide the guilty thought that she would have been happier sharing with Georgios. She put her rucksack and guitar case on the bed before opening the windows. Looking down, the narrow alley below enticingly led to the labyrinth of lanes which made up the old town.

'Why don't we unpack, then we can go out?' said Georgios reading her thoughts.

Liz sat on the single bed and emptied the scant contents of her bag. Most of her clothes were in need of a wash. She stuffed them back into her pack. Although tired from the journey she felt the thrill of anticipation at further exploring the island which she now saw in a new light. Particularly since she had met Georgios.

As they walked, Liz marvelled at the Turkish and Venetian heritage which surrounded her. Here a minaret, there a dome; tiny alleyways finding their way to open squares and a grand fountain spouting water from three lion heads which Georgios explained had been built by the Venetians as a source of clean water for the city.

Emerging at the harbourside, the view was so achingly lovely that Liz was lost for words.

'Shall we have something to eat?' Georgios asked, ushering her to a table right on the waterfront.

Liz smiled her assent before sitting and leaning back to take in the view. The coloured stuccoed buildings squeezed right up to the quayside, the view from their wooden balconies looking out onto the caiques in the harbour, the Venetian lighthouse standing at its entrance. Looking down into the water, Liz could see a shoal of fish nibbling weed from the sunken mooring ropes of the fishing boat berthed beside where they sat. The late afternoon sunshine bounced off the water, picking out the yellow, pink and honey stone and the multi-coloured awnings shading the tavernas.

Over glasses of cold beer and plates of huge prawns grilled with garlic and lemon they made plans. The following day Georgios would resume his lyra lessons with his teacher, but that was not until the evening. Until then, they had the day to themselves. If Liz did not mind riding on the back of Georgios' motorbike, he suggested they take a picnic and ride out to Arkadi monastery. As the afternoon faded into evening, Liz could not help thinking about Spinalonga. That kiss had been more than a day ago and more than one hundred miles away. As she looked at Georgios she hoped that would not be the last time he took her in his arms.

Georgios took some leftover bread from the basket, and tore it into chunks which he threw in the water causing a feeding frenzy. Liz loved the way he tried to ensure the smaller fish got food, but often they were bullied by a larger scavenger. Lights began to twinkle on the fishing boats on the quay as they were made ready for a night's fishing. A waiter brought them a plate of plump grapes, red and white, and a small carafe of raki.

'Here's to us.' Georgios leant across the table taking her hand as he raised his glass.

Liz felt a surge of excitement pass through her body at his touch. In that perfect moment she could not imagine she could ever be any happier.

Hand in hand, walking back through the old town, Liz was enchanted by the gardens hidden behind walls. In some, solitary figures sat enjoying the heady scents of the flowers which burst from containers of all shapes and sizes; others housed tavernas where diners ate noisily, enjoying the warmth of the night. From behind half-open shutters Liz could hear the sounds of food being prepared, music and even the shouts of children playing, despite the late hour.

As they moved away from the centre of the old town the alleys grew darker and Liz would have struggled to find her way through the maze of narrow lanes. She was doubly grateful that she had Georgios leading her by the hand. The darkness stirred a memory of the previous evening and, sensing her unease, Georgios put an arm around her and pulled her close. Reaching his apartment, he turned her face towards him and kissed her. In his arms she felt so different to how she had with Bob. Liz had got her wish; she would not, she suspected, be sleeping in her own room tonight and she had never felt so certain of anything she wanted more in her life.

*

Liz awoke alone to noises coming from the street below. She wrapped herself in a sheet and crossed to the already open balcony window. Looking down, she saw Georgios wheeling an old motorbike.

'I didn't want to disturb you,' he shouted up. 'I have just been out and bought some things for our picnic.' Georgios took a look at his motorbike and then up at Liz. 'Are you sure you don't mind? It goes OK, I use it to get to my uncle's farm.'

At that moment Liz would have done anything he wanted. She had never felt so in love and after the night they had spent together she was convinced that Georgios had strong feelings for her.

'Of course I'm sure, just let me shower and get dressed and we can get off as soon as you want.'

Leaving the old town, Georgios began to speed up and, with her arms clinging around her lover's waist, Liz felt a sense of exhilaration. She had never ridden on a motorbike before. In the heat of the morning sun the cooling breeze was welcome; the whole day brimmed with delicious expectation. Occasionally Georgios would turn and say something, his long hair blowing in her face as she leant into his back. Over the roar of the engine she couldn't hear what he was saying but her smile signalled to him that she was having a good time.

Inland from the national highway the going got harder and Liz had to cling on tighter as Georgios navigated the potholes in the road that wound its way into the hills. When they arrived, the splendour of the monastery made the journey worthwhile. Georgios held out his hand to help Liz dismount the bike and she felt the stiffness in her legs as she put her feet on the parched earth. As they walked towards the monastery, Georgios was almost reverential as in the shadow of the orange stone belfry he relayed the significance of this spot to Cretans and its importance in their fight against their Ottoman oppressors more than a century before.

As they crossed a cloistered courtyard shaded by vines, Georgios told her how in 1866 the monastery became the centre for resistance fighters who had risen up against their Turkish overlords, carrying out attacks on them in their stronghold in Rethymnon. Eventually the partisans were tracked down and along with their families were besieged in the monastery. Although they were vastly outnumbered, the abbot refused to surrender. Ordering the survivors of the siege to retreat into a wine store where they kept their supplies of gunpowder, as the Turks advanced he commanded that they shoot into the casks of explosives, sacrificing themselves and killing hundreds of their attackers.

Outrage at the attack on the monastery and the slaughter of so many Cretans signalled the beginning of the end of Ottoman rule. The atrocities turned the tide of international opinion against the Turks, although it took another 30 years before independence was gained. Liz could see how Georgios was moved as he stood in front of the roofless remains of the storeroom, its crumbling walls still scarred and blackened by the explosion.

An elderly monk sat sleeping on a chair outside the chapel, a cat dozing at his feet. Entering the church, Liz wondered at the paintings of the crucifixion, Adam and Eve's expulsion from the Garden of Eden, and the Burning Bush. Back outside they sat on the dusty ground eating their picnic of bread, cheese, tomatoes and olives and stared up at the foothills of the giant Psiloritis mountain range. Then, lying down with her head resting on Georgios' chest,

Liz dozed in the heat of the sun. She could have stayed there forever.

Through her dreamless slumber she heard Georgios whisper, 'We need to go now. Will you be OK in the flat alone for a couple of hours until I get back from my lesson? Then we can go to a taverna for dinner, I usually meet up with friends and we play some music.'

'I'd love that.' Liz eased herself to her feet and began to tidy up the remains of their picnic. She was looking forward to hearing Georgios play the lyra again. As they made their way down the hillside, she remembered the song she had scribbled on the piece of paper stuffed in her guitar case and from nowhere a lyric began to frame in her mind. By the time they arrived back in Rethymnon, it was almost fully formed and she could hardly wait for Georgios to leave so she could work on the song.

Sitting on the bed, she lifted her guitar and the scrappy paper from the case and picked out the melody she had written in the village. It was just as she had remembered and turning the sheet of paper over she jotted down the lyrics that had come to her on the trip down the mountainside. She had never written a song so quickly, but she sensed that it was good.

'I have no gift to give you,

So my present is this song...'

She moulded and cut the words, framing it to the melody until she knew she must stop refining or she would lose their spontaneity. By the time she heard footsteps on the stairs, she was satisfied.

'Have you been practising?' Georgios put his lyra case down and kissed her. 'Close your eyes, I have a present for you.'

Putting a small parcel into her hands, Georgios instructed, 'You can open them now.'

Looking down, Liz saw a gift-wrapped box.

'Go on, open it.'

Sliding the ribbon from the parcel, not wanting to spoil the wrapping she eased the tape off the paper. Inside was a green leather case. Opening the lid, Liz stared at an exquisite pendant of two golden bees holding a drop of honey on a gold chain.

'It's gorgeous,' she said, and putting her arms around Georgios' neck, she kissed him.

He reached into the box, unclipping the necklace. 'Turn around.' Liz touched her hand to her throat as Georgios fastened the chain around her neck.

She had never worn anything that was so stunning, she thought, lifting the necklace to see it again.

Georgios explained that it was a replica of a Minoan jewel discovered in excavations of the ancient palace of Malia.

'Will you wear it tonight to the taverna?' Liz nodded and thought she would never take it off.

'And I have a gift for you.' Sitting on the bed, she reached for her guitar and began to play.

Chapter 4

THE TAVERNA WAS packed. Some musicians were on a small dais tuning, their instruments as they drank and chatted. Holding Liz by one hand and carrying his lyra in the other, Georgios squashed his way to the stage where he left his instrument. Leading her to the side of the room he asked some friends to make space for his girlfriend. From somewhere a glass appeared and was filled with dark red wine from one of any number of jugs on the table. The air was full of the smoke of a hundred cigarettes and Georgios shouted to his friends, but Liz was unable to hear above the hubbub in the room.

Georgios seemed to know and was known by everyone and it took some time for him to make his way back to the stage and begin tuning his lyra. At the table people spoke to Liz but she understood little, her response always a smile. It was easy to feel elated as the atmosphere was charged with expectation.

As Georgios began to play, the taverna fell silent. The music curled its way into every corner of the room for a number of bars before being joined by an accompaniment played on laouto, bouzouki, guitar, fiddle and bagpipes. The connection the sound made with all in the room was palpable and Liz felt a sense of pride as she put a hand up to touch the pendant which hung at her breast.

The taverna looked too crowded for anyone to dance but somehow a space was made and dancers took to the floor, hands on each other's shoulders, the line wending its way to the square outside. As the musicians played on, Georgios wound up the tempo, and the crowd clapped and shouted. Freed from the confines of the room the lead dancer leaped slapping his heel as he hung weightless in the air. Glistening with sweat, the dancers never dropped a step as they kept up with the relentless rhythm. Just when Liz thought it could not get any faster the music reached its crescendo and stopped. For a moment there was silence before a ripple of applause turned into a tidal wave of appreciation for musicians and dancers alike.

Plates of beans, local cheese, calamari, salads and other delicious mezzes appeared from somewhere and Georgios wedged himself in beside Liz at the table. With him by her side, even in a room full of strangers, it was as though she had been coming here for all her life.

'Will you play?' As she heard Georgios' question above the animated conversation, Liz's sense of wellbeing suddenly evaporated

'Please, play the song you wrote for me. You can borrow Spyros' guitar, I'm sure.'

Liz wondered when it was she had become so frightened of performing, since the previous summer she had sung in front of large audiences and, after all, it had been her dream to become a performer. What had Georgios said to her? 'If you are a musician, you are a musician. You can never lose it. It is part of your soul.'

Taking a deep breath, Liz allowed herself to be ushered to the stage by Georgios, who stopped to ask his friend if she could use his guitar. As she settled herself on a chair and bent her ear to the body of the instrument to check the tune, she could hear Georgios introduce her. There was no going back. She began to play.

From the first note, her nerves disappeared and she let the song she had written for Georgios take her where it would. The room hushed as the soulful, plaintive ballad filled every ounce of air leaving the audience spellbound by its sublime melody.

Liz hit the final note and once again for a few seconds silence prevailed, before the crowd released the claps and cries of approval.

Flushed with pride, Georgios approached the stage and took the guitar from her hands and put it on its stand.

'That was wonderful. Thank you. And I think they liked it too,' he whispered, taking her hand and escorting her back to the table.

The fervour of the reception to her song was matched by the warmth Liz felt inside as she sat down. She found herself shaking slightly and struggled to find an anchor for her emotions. Georgios stood, bent down and kissed her before returning to the stage. The music he played was now more sombre and Liz recognised the style as the rebetika she had heard in the village. The sad and soulful melody silenced the room.

Suddenly, half a dozen beams of light invaded the inky shade of the taverna. The dazzling headlights of cars glared blindingly through the window from the square outside. The revellers who stood smoking outside the doorway were pushed roughly aside as a group of uniformed militiamen ran inside and raised their weapons. Immediately the room fell silent. Liz felt a cold shiver of fear pass through her. Forcing their way to the stage one of the militiamen grabbed Georgios by the neck while another tore the lyra from his grasp then broke it on the floor before forcing his hands behind his back and cuffing him. An old man moved to defend Georgios but was smashed in the face by the butt of a gun. Blood gushed from his nose as the man was held back by those around him.

Liz stood and opened her mouth to scream but was silenced by a uniformed thug wrenching her arms behind her back before she was bundled out of the taverna. In the square she could see Georgios being forced into one of the cars which sped away into the darkness. A hand pushed down on her and she was bent into the rear of another of the vehicles. She raised her head to protest but was silenced by what caught her eye standing in the shadows, the unmistakable sinister figure in a long coat.

'What are you doing? Where are you taking him?' Liz screamed in the face of a policeman who cuffed her hand to his in the back of the car.

'He is going somewhere where he will get the chance to admit he is wrong to play such music. If he is persuaded to learn this, he may be set free. If not,' the man shrugged, 'who knows. Some people never learn that they have to obey the rules. And foreigners like you should learn to keep out of the affairs of our country.'

The cramp in her arm was nothing to the fear she felt for Georgios as the car drove out of the square only to stop a minute later outside Georgios' apartment. She could see the door had been smashed in already and she was taken upstairs where the handcuffs were taken off and she was instructed to pack her bag while the policeman stood guard over her. Through the open door of Georgios' flat, she could see it had been ransacked, and her guitar that she had left in his room had been smashed on the tiled floor. She felt a torrent of anger but fear held her back. With her belongings stuffed in her rucksack she made to retrieve the remains of her guitar, but was roughly pulled away from the doorway and down the stairs into the police car and handcuffed again to the guard.

Leaving behind the lights of the city they sped through the darkness, twisting and turning on the mountain roads. Every so often Liz could sense the vast void of the sea beside them. Tonight it had changed from the boundless blue of possibilities to a menacing, invisible, oily presence. She realised they were travelling on the national highway, retracing the route she had taken on the bus the previous day. Then she had been filled with hope and anticipation; now all she felt was terror at the thought of what would happen to Georgios and herself. She tried to speak to the guard and the driver but her words were met with silence and she was left with only her petrified thoughts for company.

She lost track of time, and although mentally exhausted she had never been more wide awake when she saw the lights of the city ahead. She was back in Heraklion. Along the sea front she recognised the harbour wall with the fort silhouetted against the ink black of the sea. Opposite the old harbour, beside the crumbling walls of the Venetian arsenals, the driver swung the car off the road. Taking her rucksack from the boot he pushed her up the outside stairs of a forbidding building. Still handcuffed, Liz was marshalled into a first-floor room, dimly lit by one bare light bulb. She let her eyes adjust.

The room had the acrid smell of sweat. Behind a desk sat a fat, uniformed man perspiring heavily. His jacket undone, Liz could see the damp spreading across his crumpled shirt from beneath his arms, one of which was embellished with a gold lanyard. The desk was empty save for a single piece of paper, a belt with a holstered pistol and a royal blue cap.

The policeman reached inside her bag and pulled out her passport and air ticket and put them on the desk. The fat man opened a drawer and pulled out an inkpad and stamp before opening the passport and putting an official mark on a blank page and writing over it in pen.

'You will be leaving us tonight... and not coming back. The flight to Athens will be courtesy of us and my man will escort you to see you get on a plane from there to London. You will never be returning. We don't have time to make friends with foreigners.' The obese man's English was fluent but menacing. 'We will be spending a little more time with your boyfriend so we can get better acquainted.

'We like to make sure all our people are friends.' His smile sent a shudder through Liz. 'Those who come to visit us usually leave as friends. It will be his choice.'

She opened her mouth to speak but no words would come. She was frozen with fear. Before she could muster her courage, she was pushed through the door back down to the car that had brought her there.

In the early hours of the morning the airport at Heraklion was empty. Under the guard of the same special policeman she was ushered through the usual baggage and security checks to a small windowless room. Alone with her thoughts, she was torn: fearful for her own life, she could not help feeling a sense of relief to be getting away; but that made the remorse that she would never see Georgios again almost unbearable. She told herself there was nothing she could do to help her lover but the guilt still lingered. She was relieved when the door opened and she was taken outside. The night air was hot and sticky as she was walked across the runway to an Olympic Airways plane. Climbing the stairs, she was the first aboard and was seated alongside her guard at the rear of the aircraft, well away from the few passengers who were taking the early morning flight to the capital.

Sitting in silence, Liz was alone with thoughts which would not settle in her head. Although it was cold in the cabin of the aircraft she could feel herself sweating. She was grateful when she felt the plane begin its descent towards the lights of the city.

Landing in Athens, they waited until the passengers had got off before descending the steps to the tarmac, where a police car awaited to transport them to the international airport. Here she was escorted onto another aircraft where she was uncuffed. Liz felt some release at being alone, but as she looked down from the window of the plane she could see the policeman awaiting the aircraft's departure.

With the other passengers boarded and the cabin doors closed, as the plane began to taxi towards the runway the tears began to roll down Liz's cheeks. A mixture of anger at what had happened, relief at her escape and fear for the future of Georgios all surged out. Seeing her distress, a member of the cabin crew brought her water and some tissues. Liz knew the woman would be aware of her deportation and was grateful for her friendly face and comforting words.

As the plane rose into the air, the sun came up and looking down, Liz couldn't reconcile the beauty of the land beneath her with the ugly, brutal regime that held sway there. She could not get out of her mind the lurking figure of Stelios, and feared for Anna.

Was the imprisonment of Georgios to be his only revenge for Anna's rejection of his advances? And how could the playing of music be the pretext for her lover's arrest and her ejection from Greece? She thought back to the first time she had heard Georgios play rebetika on the terrace of his parents' house up the mountainside from Elounda. Anna had told her they were songs of freedom and that musicians had been tortured for playing them. In Stelios' twisted mind, had that been the excuse he used to get revenge for his humiliation?

Emotionally exhausted, in the moments she dozed Liz could forget her living nightmare, but as her spinning thoughts awakened her she realised it was all too real. She was on her way to a country where she had little to return to. She had burned her boats when she left university and had become estranged from both her separated parents. The guilt she had felt at the breakdown of her mum and dad's marriage began to seep back, making her feel hopeless. But that desperation was far better than the brutality of the regime she was escaping.

Crossing the Alps, the plane bucked in turbulence and Liz thought of the man she was leaving behind. She had known him for less than a week but in that short time she had fallen in love. She was scared to think where Georgios was now or if he was even still alive, and now she would never be allowed to return to discover his fate. Anna had told her Georgios would never recant the beliefs expressed in the songs of freedom, but surely he would not sacrifice his life for the music he so loved?

The mountains seemed far below, the world tiny in comparison with the thoughts she wrestled with. The plane plummeted as it hit a hollow pocket in the sky before finding the air to buoy it up. For a moment the fear distracted from her dark thoughts about Georgios. Leaving the Alps behind the turbulence eased but Liz could not shake the turmoil inside her head.

Liz closed her eyes as she heard the landing gear crank from the housings beneath the wings. She swallowed hard as the aircraft twitched, dropping height and speed. A bump and the reverse thrust of the engines signalled they were on the ground. Through the window, Liz gazed out at the wet mid-morning that awaited her. She sat until the other passengers had disembarked, before reaching up to take her pack from the locker and leaving the plane.

Following the crowd, she walked through the soulless tunnels towards passport control. Surely someone would want to question her about what had happened? On showing her passport she was nodded through by the officer and the customs hall was empty. In no time she found herself exiting into the arrivals lounge. Families rushed to cuddle their loved ones and taxi drivers held up cards with customer names scribbled on them.

Liz stopped and looked around. She could hardly believe that events so cataclysmic to her could go unnoticed by the rest of the world. She sat down on a seat in the terminal to contemplate her situation and try to focus on what to do. Involuntarily she reached for the pendant around her neck, the two bees harvesting a sweet drop of honey. Somehow the necklace reassured her that she would always have a connection with the man who had given her the gift and who she loved so much. She remembered the moment when he had given it to her the previous evening, how she had felt his warm breath on her neck as he had fastened the clasp. That now seemed a lifetime ago. She thought about how she had in return played the song she had written for him and the sparkle of delight she had noticed in his deep brown eyes as she plucked the strings.

In the world of the here and now Liz could find little consolation. She cast her mind back to her childhood. Had her parents not always cared for her, loved and supported her? Had she given them the help and support they needed when she discovered their relationship was going through a rocky patch? When she had left England for Greece she had not even let them know. She realised that she must have hurt them, but that was what she had wanted to do in her anger at their separation.

Searching in her purse for the right coins, she found a public telephone, took a deep breath and dialled the number. Her mother answered and on hearing Liz's voice burst into tears. Liz too found the emotion of speaking to her mum too much to bear and she could not stop herself from crying. In between the apologies and reassurances Liz was told to go straight to her family home, where she could stay for as long as she wanted.

Finding a bureau de change, Liz cashed a traveller's cheque for sterling before following the signs for the shuttle bus service and heading into central London to get the connection from Waterloo to Salisbury. As the train pulled out of the London terminus on the last leg of her journey she felt a longing to see her mother. After all that had happened in the previous 24 hours she realised the familiarity of home might bring some comfort after all.

Chapter 5

IT WAS EVENING when Liz stepped off the train in the Wiltshire city she had known since childhood. She remembered how most weekends her parents would drive there from the village where they lived to do the weekly shop and often they would go for lunch together before returning home. How far away it seemed from that other city, Rethymnon, where just the evening before, the malign events had unfolded that had returned her here. Liz shuddered as she thought of Georgios alone at the mercy of the brutal thugs who had arrested him.

The taxi driver took her rucksack and put it in the boot of his cab and they set off towards the village. In the dusk she could see the ancient boulders of Stonehenge silhouetted against the flame-red sun as it disappeared over the plain. She had seen the monument so many times before, but that evening it was a reassuring presence as they drove the narrow roads which criss-crossed the chalkland downs.

As they drew up outside the house, the front door was thrown open. Liz stepped out of the taxi and was smothered in her mother's hug. By the time she had found money in her purse her mother had already paid the driver, picked up the bag and was leading her inside.

Whilst her mother fussed around making sandwiches and uncorking a bottle of wine, Liz sank into the deep comfort of the familiar sofa, exhausted, relieved yet distraught. She had exchanged one sense of guilt for another: having patched things up with her mother, she now felt remorse at how she had escaped the fate she feared Georgios was suffering.

It helped no end to open up to her mother. Until she had left for university they had always been good friends. They talked long into the night and Liz was overjoyed when her mum revealed that there was a chance that her parents might get back together. Mother and daughter apologised for the hurt they had done to each other and Liz described the events that had befallen her in Crete. As she spoke from the luxury of the chintz sofa, she felt a sense of detachment from a situation which yesterday had seemed only too real.

Now she was back in her family home, her mother reassured her that she could stay as long as she wanted. Maybe she could reapply for university, restart her course in the autumn and begin playing gigs again to rebuild her music career. Her mother's offers of support were a comfort which lay at odds with the despair she felt about the bleak future facing the man she loved.

It was almost 11 o'clock by the time Liz awoke the following morning. She came down from her bedroom to find her father waiting for her in the kitchen. She could see the joy on his face at seeing her and feel the reassurance of his arms around her as they hugged. From her mother's smile she could tell her parents were relaxed around each other and heard the affection in their voices as they spoke together.

'Your mother phoned and told me you were home and all about what happened to you in Crete. We thought we might take you out, didn't we Sue, maybe buy you a new guitar and get some lunch?'

The thought of going shopping again in the city with her parents filled Liz with a warm feeling. 'I would love that! Just give me time to get showered. Are my old clothes still in the wardrobe in my room?'

'Of course.' Her mother smiled.

Under the powerful shower, Liz scrubbed away the dirt of the previous day and washed her tangled hair. She unearthed some jeans and a t-shirt from the wardrobe and when she had finished dressing she let herself for a moment forget what had happened to her. She instinctively realised that for her own sanity she would have to start to erase those memories but knew in her heart that, for however long she lived, they would never escape her.

In the music shop in Salisbury, her father Paul was keen that his daughter try all the guitars. To him, whichever one she played sounded marvellous, but he was content to be patient and waited with his wife until Liz found her perfect choice.

'What do you think of this one?' Liz held up an exquisite guitar in both hands, its front a light spruce contrasting with a back and sides in dark walnut. 'It's quite expensive.'

'I'm sure your father won't mind what it costs.' Susan raised an eyebrow at her husband, who turned over the price ticket hanging from the neck of the instrument.

'Of course I don't mind. That's fine.'

Liz sat down in the shop and turned the tuning keys before sitting down to play. The song that came out was the one she had written for her lover back in Crete. As soon as she played the opening notes she was transported by her own tune, softly humming the melody to accompany the song. The guitar was much better than the one that had been smashed to pieces by the fascists in Crete. Looking up, she saw her father squeeze her mum's hand.

'That's beautiful, darling. Is it a tune you wrote?'

Liz nodded. 'It's just perfect; if you are sure it's OK?' She held the guitar out to her father.

'Yes, and we need a case, and all the other bits and bobs, what do you call it, a capo and the like.' Paul said to the saleswoman.

Returning to the car to put their purchases in the boot, they went for lunch at the restaurant they had visited so often before she had left home. With her parents together it was as if the clock had been wound back. Liz recounted the story of her time in Crete to her father, and could see the concern on his face as she told of her treatment at the hands of the special police. Although the memory was still raw, it helped Liz to unburden herself by telling the story, but she could not avoid dark thoughts about what the future held for Georgios.

In the days that followed, Liz found herself playing guitar or walking in the spring sunshine on the plain. Out in the open air she could sometimes slam the door shut on the darkened room in her head where her memories of those final days in Crete languished. She found joy in rediscovering her love of music and hope in her thoughts of performing again. She noticed that her father and mother were spending more time in each other's company and, as the days turned into weeks, if she had not forgotten what had happened in Crete, at least she could for moments push it to the back of her mind.

It was some weeks later that Liz realised she had missed her period. A trip to the doctor confirmed her thoughts, she was pregnant. Leaving the GP's surgery, her mind was everywhere. She loved Georgios but, even if he was still alive, she had no way of letting him know he was to be a father. She could never return to Crete. What would her parents think and how could she look after a baby and go back to university and pursue her career? But inside she knew despite all these things that she was overjoyed to be carrying the baby of the man she loved. Whatever had happened to Georgios, a part of him would live on through his child.

She plucked up the courage and told her parents that same afternoon. Any misgivings she may have had were swept away when she saw the delight on their faces at the prospect of becoming grandparents. They hugged and kissed her and promised all the love and help they could give.

Liz's parents gave her any support they could. It seemed as though her unborn child had brought them closer together again and it was not long before her father had moved back into the family home. They both promised that they would help to look after the child while Liz returned to university and when she was playing gigs. Her father even suggested that Liz should try and write to Anna to see if she had any news of Georgios.

With the houses having no numbers and the alleys having no names, Liz addressed her letter just to Anna's name and the village. As the weeks went by she longed for a response, but heard nothing from her friend. She wrote again, and still got no answer. As her bump began to show, she decided to try sending a letter to the local kafenio to pass on to Anna. It was a long shot and Liz remembered the woman who owned it spoke no English, but she was kindly and maybe would get the letter to Anna.

Nearly a month later, Liz was sitting at the kitchen table when her mother handed her a letter from Greece. Her heart skipped a beat. Almost afraid to open it, she slowly tore the top off the envelope. As she read her eyes welled up with tears. She had been right to put faith in the woman, who had given her letter to a friend of Georgios and Anna's family in the village to respond.

The news was not good. Not long after Georgios' arrest, a gloating Stelios had visited the family home in the village. He could hardly conceal his delight at torturing Anna with the news that her brother had died in custody. The family, distraught, in danger and unable to see any future under the brutal regime, had fled the country for Australia. Nobody in the village had heard from them since.

Liz was sobbing; she remembered what the fat military policeman had said to her in that murky room in Heraklion the night they had been arrested. 'Those who come to visit us usually leave as friends. It will be his choice.' From the short time she had known Georgios she thought she knew what he would choose, and that he would have paid the price for such courage with his life.

The memories of that fateful night returned and threw a dark shadow over Liz's thoughts through which she could see no future. Little her parents could say to her at that moment could heal the pain. She spent the rest of the day and the following night in bed. Even when she fell into exhausted sleep there was no relief, as her dreams were nightmares and she could not find a way through the darkness which smothered her thoughts. Sometime just before dawn was breaking she fell asleep and when she awoke she felt as though she had no more grief, her face taut and exhausted when she forced herself out of bed. From somewhere in the night, though, she had found a new determination. She would love her child like no other, and through the baby, Georgios would live on, a tribute to their love for one another and his bravery.

She crossed the room and picked up her guitar from its stand in the corner, then returned to sit on the bed. She drew her fingers across the strings and her hand danced over the frets as she played the song she had written for her now dead lover. Inside her she felt the baby kick.

Chapter 6

LIZ SPENT THE summer days of her early pregnancy walking on Salisbury Plain, playing her guitar and meeting up with old friends from school. She felt nothing but happiness about the unborn child inside her which eased the pain when her thoughts spread to Georgios. Her parents were closer than ever, and she laughed at their excitement as they emptied the box room in their house and decorated and furnished it as a nursery.

Despite her parents' offers of help, Liz would not entertain the thought of returning to her studies. She knew she had to devote her energy and love to the care of her child. She was asked to play some gigs in local pubs, which she did with pleasure and a lack of inhibition she had not felt before. Stripped of all ambition, her music soared with an authenticity which touched the hearts of her small audiences drinking on a Saturday night.

As summer turned into autumn Liz's bump grew bigger. Although she was on the verge of becoming a mother herself, the care and love of her parents took her back to her childhood days. As the leaves turned bronze on the trees and began to drop they made turnip lanterns, and the fireworks on Guy Fawkes' Night sparked memories of that Easter when she had first met Georgios.

Christmas was magical. Liz helped her father decorate the tree, although he refused to let her climb on a chair to put the angel on top. They made Christmas pudding and iced a cake, cooked ham and made a large pork pie. Friends came round for a party on Christmas Eve and on Christmas morning Liz woke up to find a stocking filled with gifts at the end of her bed: a tin of plectrums, guitar strings, sleep suits for the baby, and an orange.

Downstairs her father was busy peeling potatoes and preparing vegetables, the delicious smell of the turkey already cooking in the oven. When the preparations for lunch were done, he turned his attention to preparing a breakfast of scrambled eggs and smoked salmon.

Presents around the tree followed: records, books, a teddy bear and clothes for the baby. Liz's parents had done everything they could to make the day special. She felt loved and secure and was looking forward to the day she could hold the baby in her arms. She found comfort in her music, particularly in the song she had written for her lover back in Crete. Whilst her parents cleared away the dishes after Christmas dinner, Liz escaped upstairs to her room and began to play. Sitting on the bed, tears rolled down her cheeks as she picked out the notes and quietly sang. A heady mix of emotions about the day, her baby, and Georgios welled up inside her.

'That was beautiful, why don't you come downstairs and play?' Liz heard her mother's comforting tones at her bedroom door.

Putting her arm around Liz, her mother shepherded her downstairs to the sitting room where a fire had been lit in the grate. As she sat playing the guitar and staring into the coals, the time Liz had spent on Crete drifted into the distant past.

In the days that followed they took walks out in the countryside, the crisp ground crunching beneath their feet and their warm breath steaming in the cold winter air. On the afternoon of New Year's Eve, Liz felt the pain of her contractions and was rushed to hospital in Salisbury, where after a long labour she gave birth to a baby girl. Some weeks premature, she was small but healthy and in Liz's eyes perfect in every way.

From the moment she was born, Phoebe was wrapped in the warm blanket of her mother's love and the comforting support of her adoring grandparents. If at times Liz let her mind drift back to the tragedy of Crete she would remind herself that Georgios lived on through his daughter and she was determined to give all the love she could muster to their child.

Chapter 7

'LEAVE HER YOU bastards!' As the police car sped out of the square, Georgios looked back to see Liz being manhandled into another vehicle. He tried to struggle but in handcuffs he was easily overpowered by his guard who forced his head forwards onto his knees.

Georgios felt helpless as he was driven through the dark streets of the old city. The pain in his back and neck could not take away from the agony he was feeling at the arrest of his lover. He had been stupid to underestimate the malice of the Junta towards the music he loved and that misjudgement had put Liz's life in danger. Now she was alone, frightened and in the hands of the violent thugs who ruled his homeland. The fear he felt for Liz at that moment far outweighed any concerns he had for his own fate.

His eyes adjusted slowly to the darkness of the damp stone cell they slung him in. He knew he was still in Rethymnon from the short time he had been in the police car, but there was no window in the tiny room from which he could see out. The dank air pressed on his thoughts. There was no bed. Exhausted he sat on the floor, his back against the bare walls. For hours he drifted in and out of sleep, not knowing whether it was day or night. Asleep or awake he could not escape the horror in which he found himself. Although he had only known her for a few days, he knew he was in love with Liz and she had been snatched away from him, her life endangered by his other love, that of his music.

*

'Your foreign whore has been sent back where she belongs.' Sneering with hate the crisp-shirted officer spat out his words. 'You however will be staying with us. For how long, it is up to you.'

Standing, the uniformed militiaman pushed a piece of paper across the table between them. 'Sign this now and all the unpleasantness could soon be over. If not, we might need to educate you in what we expect from a true citizen of our homeland.'

Georgios looked down at the paper and read the short statement he was being asked to sign. Just the squiggle of a pen and he could be free. All he had to do was to sign a statement saying that he would not play such music again and pledge allegiance to the regime. He pushed the paper back towards the uniformed man. If he signed he knew he would never be free again. To signal his support for a government that had abducted the woman that he loved and forbade the playing of the music that was his passion would have driven him mad with guilt. Liz had been deported from the country so at least he knew she would be safe; as for himself, he would have to dig deep into his inner strength.

'When will you people learn that we will not tolerate anything that undermines what makes Greece great!' Georgios could not help noticing the spittle which had formed in the corner of the mouth of the man who was now shouting at him. 'Take him back to his cell.'

*

Emerging briefly into the sunlight, Georgios could not fathom how long he had been kept in the damp hell hole. But his sight of the clear blue sky was short lived as he was forced by an armed guard into the back of a military truck. Through the flap in the canvas covering, tantalising glimpses of light seeped in on a welcome breath of fresh air. The familiar scents of mountain herbs mingled with the smell of sweat and diesel fumes under the tarpaulin as the lorry bumped its way in what Georgios realised was a westerly direction. His guard, dressed in army fatigues, looked bored but was armed with a rifle and Georgios' hands were cuffed in front of him. For a moment the small pleasure he felt at being free of his cell was imbued with foreboding at what lay ahead.

The truck came to a halt and he could hear the driver conversing with another man before they moved slowly forward again, navigating around the grid of streets of what seemed to be a military base. When they came to a halt, his guard signalled for him to climb down. On another day in another time, Georgios would have been entranced by the view which greeted him. Momentarily he looked out on a vast natural harbour cradled by wooded hillsides and bare rocks tumbling down into the sea while, in the distance, small islands floated at the wide mouth of the bay. He was standing on a quayside. A push in the back steered him towards the edge, where his handcuffs were removed and he was told to descend a ladder down the seafront wall onto a small boat. Stepping aboard the craft, his hands were secured again by another guard. Georgios watched as the fore and aft mooring ropes were cast off by the crew and the boat headed seawards, and he wondered if he would ever see his homeland again.

Looking out into the bay, Georgios could see a large grey warship at anchor in the straits. The tender pulled alongside and was made fast at the bottom of the side of the hull which towered above them. A hatch was cranked open and Georgios was forced up a ladder and through it into the bowels of the ship, where he was led through a maze of corridors before being shoved into a bare cabin on which a heavy steel door was slammed shut. The ominous thudding of the idle engines was Georgios' only companion as he settled into his cramped quarters. The noise got louder, accompanied by the sound of winches hauling on fathoms of anchor chain, signalling the ship was about to sail. Georgios was certain in his mind they were moored in Souda Bay, but to where the ship was heading he had no inkling.

The cabin was airless and stiflingly hot and, as the ship left the shelter of the harbour for the open sea, the pitching motion when it drove through the waves made settling impossible. Starving, tired and dirty, it seemed as though his imprisonment had already lasted an eternity. His lonely mind threw around what horrors the future might hold and however he tried he could not shake these thoughts.

The throb of the engines drummed out the beat to this never-ending symphony of anguish as the hours went by. Once the door was opened and a piece of bread and a glass of water were placed inside before it was slammed shut again. Was it better that this journey should last forever and he would never discover his fate?

He could feel the engines slow and the anchors drop as the ship made harbour. The wait seemed unending before the door was opened and he was escorted through the corridors and companionways of the ship before emerging at a hatch near the waterline where another tender awaited. There he was pulled aboard by some guards before the smaller boat was cast off and headed to what Georgios could discern was an island.

As they neared the shore he could make out the barbed wire fences and watchtowers guarding over the most austere building Georgios had ever seen. Even its exterior was a crime against all things human. Such brutality could mask nothing good inside. The lines from the boat were thrown ashore and made fast around the rusting iron bollards on the desolate quay. Looking up, he saw the familiar red-and-black flag flying on a pole above the huge bleak building, a stain on an otherwise perfect blue sky.

Pushed inside the prison gates, the sky was gone and the smell of despair hit him like a baton as he was marched past ranks of steel doors muffling the sounds of pain and smell of fear within. Georgios felt a shudder pass through his body as he was deposited in a tiny cell, a bucket his only companion. How had he got to this? He let his mind drift back to the night he had been arrested, to Liz and the music they loved. He knew that he could never renounce all that was good in the world.

It was hours later, he did not know how many, that Georgios was marshalled into a large office. A window looked out onto barbed wire and bare brick walls, the domain of the man who sat behind an antique desk. In another context the furniture might have hinted at sophistication, but that was obviously alien to this man filled only with salivating self-satisfaction. The governor oozed the intimidation of his stock in trade. 'Welcome to Gyaros.'

The name of the island was familiar to Georgios as a place of exile; it had a grim history as a prison as recently as Greece's civil war. That the barbaric heritage of this small Cycladic island had been preserved by the Junta came as no surprise to Georgios.

'This is the last time you will be asked to sign this, without some encouragement.' Reaching in a desk drawer he pulled out a file, took out the single page document Georgios had refused to sign in Rethymnon and slid it over the desk, throwing a pen down on top of it.

Georgios searched for a response but could not find words to express his feelings of contempt, loathing and fear. For what seemed like minutes he stood silent.

'You leave me no choice.' Clicking his tongue, the governor raised his head in a gesture to the guards and Georgios was pulled towards the door.

The torturers wasted no time getting to work on Georgios. They chained him down and beat him on the feet with batons until he passed out with the pain, when they would throw a bucket of water over his body to revive him. This *falanga* punishment was favoured as, over time, it left few visible scars but for prisoners like

Georgios who would not succumb it was rarely enough. In frustration the torturers would beat and kick the unconscious body before having it dragged to the hospital wing.

When Georgios came round for the first time in those unfamiliar surroundings, agony wracked his body and his vision was blurred.

'He's awake.' He heard a woman's voice before seeing the shadow of a man's face over him.

'We must change his dressings before they discover he has come round and take him back to his cell.' The man spoke to the nurse before whispering to Georgios. 'I am Dimitris, the doctor here. Like you I am a prisoner, but they find it useful to set me to work keeping people alive so they can torture them more.'

The doctor told Georgios that he was badly bruised and had two broken fingers as well as the severe bruising to his feet. Dimitris had been right and later Georgios was dragged back to his cell where he languished until the next day, when he was taken away again to be tortured. The pain was almost unbearable, but from somewhere Georgios found the inner strength to fight the agony until his body gave out.

As the weeks went by he would fool the guards by pretending not to come round so that he was taken to the hospital, if only for a few hours. He valued the human company and as time went on became a friend of the doctor who was so kind to him. Knowing he might see Dimitris added to Georgios' determination not to buckle under the relentless torture.

Each time the guards would arrive to take Georgios back to his cell, Dimitris would warn them that Georgios' body could not take much more. In the few hours they had together, Dimitris would talk about his wife Eleni who had been pregnant with his unborn child when he had been arrested for treating a man who was considered an enemy of the state. His child should now have been born and he hoped was living safely on the island of Rhodes with Eleni.

Spending time with the doctor, Georgios began to notice that Dimitris was himself unwell. Sometimes he would turn away from his patient and cough into a filthy handkerchief which was stained with blood. He asked his friend about his health, whereupon the doctor confessed that he had tuberculosis, which was getting steadily worse in the harsh conditions of the prison.

Georgios lost track of how long the days of beatings lasted, but one day he was taken from his cell and instead of the torture chamber he was set to hard labour breaking rocks with a group of prisoners who had all frustrated the attempts of their captors to shatter their resolve. The days were long and hard, but at least Georgios was outside and although at first his body was in agony from the punishment it had taken, over the weeks it gained in strength from the hard physical labour.

Anything was better than the torture he had suffered from the sadistic bullies who had tried to make him conform to their twisted doctrine but if Georgios missed one thing it was seeing Dimitris. He had seen men collapse from exhaustion from the heavy work they were forced to do in the heat of the sun with no shade and little water. Faking his own collapse was not difficult and a failure to be revived by baton blows and buckets of cold water resulted in his body being dragged to the hospital wing. Since he had seen him last, Dimitris looked diminished, his cheeks hollow and his body weak. His pleasure at seeing Georgios could not disguise his frailty.

As they talked, Dimitris expressed his fears that he had not long to live, and for the future of his family. In that moment Georgios made a promise that if he ever got through this ordeal he would seek them out and help in whatever way he could.

'Thank you, my friend,' were the last words Georgios ever heard Dimitris speak as he held onto his hand before the guards returned Georgios to his cell. Some days later, a fellow labourer taken to the hospital ward had been treated by the nurse, who told him the doctor had passed away. If there ever was an end to this hell he was living through, Georgios knew he must honour his pledge to Dimitris.

If only the doctor could have held out a bit longer he might have been saved. When the end to the horrors of imprisonment came, it came quickly. Unbeknown to the prisoners, following the debacle when the Junta failed to prevent a Turkish invasion of Cyprus, the regime crumbled and a request was sent out to the former Prime Minister, Konstantinos Karamanlis, to return from exile in Paris to take up the reins of government.

Only days after Karamanlis set foot on Greek soil the military guards fled and boats arrived to liberate the prisoners from the prison island. Along with many other inmates who had been held on Gyaros, Georgios was taken to Athens by ship. There his experiences at the hands of the regime were documented and he was given a small amount of drachma to help him on his way. He desperately wanted to return to his family on Crete but had not forgotten the promise he had made to Dimitris.

At the bustling port of Piraeus, he found a ship to take him to Rhodes. Sleeping on deck, Georgios revelled in the sense of freedom as the ferry pushed south from the capital. At last sailing around the ancient fortress town of Rhodes, the ship found dock in the shadow of the city walls.

In the seaside village of Charaki on the eastern coast of Rhodes where the doctor's wife had sought sanctuary, Georgios went in search of Eleni and her child to tell her of her husband's passing. But the news he discovered was tragic. Eleni had now been reunited with her husband in death, as she had died giving birth to a baby boy just three months earlier. Making inquiries with the local priest, Georgios discovered that the child, after being baptised, had been put into the care of an orphanage to the south of the island.

With the orphanage overwhelmed in the wake of the recent bloody dictatorship, it did not take much for Georgios to persuade them to release the child, who had been named Andreas, into his care. He was sure that with the help of his family he could fulfil the commitment he had made to the doctor.

The following day he secured a passage on a ferry for Crete, departing two days later. Renting a room in the old town, Georgios spent the time struggling to get to grips with catering for the needs of a baby. In between feeding and changing his young charge, when the boy was not sleeping Georgios carried Andreas with him to stock up on essentials he would need for their journey.

The seas were calm and the gentle motion of the ship as it headed south to Crete seemed to comfort the child who only awoke to be fed, the rest of the time sleeping in the balmy heat on a makeshift bed made from towels and clothes Georgios had managed to buy with the few drachma he had been given.

Stepping off the ferry at Heraklion, Georgios felt a sense of elation at his return to a place he at one time thought he may never see again. The people on the quayside meeting friends and relatives shouted and waved, the joy of their newly found freedom etched on their faces. Cradling the baby in his arms, he boarded a bus east towards Agios Nikolaos. The familiar places they passed, he now saw through new eyes. How he had missed the scents, sights and sounds of his homeland. In Agios Nikolaos he boarded a bus for Elounda and as it crested the hill at Lenika his heart leaped at the site of the bay of Korfos and the island of Spinalonga keeping watch over the northern approaches.

Before his walk up the mountainside to the village, Georgios stopped for a drink and to change and feed the baby. Elounda was quiet in the heat of the afternoon sun but a taverna on the square was open and he sat himself in the shade of a tree outside. At first the owner didn't recognise Georgios, his unkempt hair and long beard disguising his looks.

In the moment of recognition the man instinctively smiled. Then his expression changed to one of shock. Georgios could sense that something was wrong. The owner of the taverna sat at the table and recounted how Anna and his parents had been visited by Stelios who, not satisfied with getting Georgios arrested and his girlfriend deported, had told them that he had been executed for crimes against the state.

103

In their grief, the family had left everything behind to start a new life in Australia. The house in the village was as they had left it, but nobody had heard from them since. Some weeks after their hasty departure the decomposing body of Stelios was found on the mountainside still dressed in his long coat, a bullet wound to the head. The military police had tried to no avail to discover his murderer. It could have been anyone in the village who had pulled the trigger. Hearing the news about his family, Georgios had never felt so alone as he did sitting there with the small child in his care.

The trek up the donkey path was filled with the pain of not being able to see his family again. As he reached the outskirts of the village some neighbours peeked out from behind shutters, others nodded to Georgios, too embarrassed to speak. Under a rock beside the front door to his parents' house he found the key which had always been kept there. Inside, apart from the accumulation of dust, the house was much as it had been when he had left that day for Rethymnon with Liz.

A tear came to his eye at the memory, but a cry from Andreas demanded his attention. After the child's immediate needs had been met, Georgios took a drawer from the dresser and lined it with a pillow covered in pieces of sheet he cut from some clean bedding and put Andreas down to sleep. Opening the door to the terrace, he sat outside staring down the hillside to the bay below. How, he wondered, could somewhere so sublime, be the place which had caused him so much pain?

He looked out at his parents' olive grove, which had been in the family for generations. Now that branch had been snapped and he realised he was unlikely to see his family again. Suddenly fatigue and the pain of all he had lost came over him and he fell into troubled sleep. When he awoke in the first light of the new day, through his fitful dreams he had resolved one thing: he could not remain in the village with all the memories that it held for him.

He stretched and went inside, warmed some milk and fed the baby before taking him in his arms. Locking the front door, he put the key back under the rock and headed down the mountainside.

Chapter 8

WHEN SHE WAS old enough, Liz was honest with her daughter about her father. She told her how she had fallen in love with Georgios while she was on Crete and that he had died, although spared her the detail of his demise. The girl seemed carefree and had the happiest of childhoods brought up by her mother and grandparents. After Phoebe went to school, Liz was keen to contribute more to the household and began to teach guitar from the family home. Playing music again was a real joy for Liz, but nothing compared to the love she felt daily when she saw Phoebe running towards her as she waited at the school gates.

Phoebe loved nothing better than to be outside, playing in the garden of her grandparents' house and, walking for miles with their black Labrador on Salisbury Plain. She was slow to read and although attentive at school she struggled to keep up with the more academic children. But she was happy, and for her mother that was all that mattered. From an early age Phoebe would dance ceaselessly to records played on her grandparents' record player and, as the years passed, tried to emulate her mother by strumming her guitar. Liz had unending patience and encouraged her interest, Phoebe's love of music echoing her own passion.

For her sixth birthday her grandparents bought her a quarter-size guitar. From the moment Phoebe unwrapped her present, clicked open the case and eased the instrument from its cushion of blue velvet she was captivated. That very day her mother showed her the shapes of some basic chords and in the days and weeks that followed, when Phoebe had come home from school, they would sit for hours learning songs.

From early on it was obvious that Phoebe had a talent and loved playing so much that she was glad to practice in any spare moment she had. It was not long before mother and daughter were performing impromptu concerts for Sue and Paul in the living room, the proud grandparents overjoyed at how Phoebe took them back to the days when Liz had been her age.

Phoebe would sit at the old upright piano and soon taught herself to play, but it was the guitar that she loved and she would practise for hours in her room, perfecting the songs her mother had taught her. She experimented with styles and when she moved to the comprehensive school she was bought an electric guitar and amplifier by her mother. Every Saturday she was driven to Salisbury by her mum and, while Liz went shopping, Phoebe would take lessons with a teacher in the city.

Phoebe loved the freedom the electric instrument gave her, its volume, versatility and the sounds she could squeeze from the speakers, but it was to the acoustic guitar that she returned when she needed to be alone and, as her creativity took flight, to write her own songs. Her talent made her popular at school, and her teachers were pleased she had found a way to progress through her music. As Phoebe moved into her teens, Liz would ferry her daughter around to various local venues where she would play in bands or sing alone with her guitar. All the time Liz would burst with pride at hearing her daughter play and only sometimes did she feel a sense of loss at the career she might have had.

Liz still cherished the moments they spent playing guitar together and Phoebe had added a number of her mother's own songs to her repertoire. All, in fact, except one. Liz had resisted teaching Phoebe the song she had written for her father. It was not that she was holding back from her daughter, but she felt the song was intensely personal. Teaching it to her daughter could wait until Liz felt she was old enough to hear the whole truth about Georgios.

When Phoebe was 14 and navigating the difficult course of her adolescent years, Liz could detect in the music her daughter was writing that her mind had turned to more adult themes. Phoebe showed some reluctance to play some of the new songs she had written, and Liz sensed the embarrassment the young woman was feeling in giving away too much of herself through her music.

'It is only when you are honest in your songs that they will be great,' Liz reassured her daughter. 'I know how difficult that is, but if your music is true to yourself, then people will love it.'

Liz then picked up her guitar. It had been many years since she had played the song she had written for Georgios. At first she thought she might have forgotten it, but as soon as she picked the first notes it came back to her, as fresh as it was all those years ago in Crete. Thoughts of that precious time she had spent with the man she loved came flooding back. Holding back the tears, she channelled her emotions into the song. It had stood the test of time and, suffused with the passions brought to the fore by those bitter-sweet memories, the song had a power that reached into Phoebe's soul.

'That is beautiful. I've never heard it before.' Phoebe looked questioningly at her mother.

'I wrote it for your father.' Liz dropped her head, as a wave of sadness suddenly washed over her.

'Tell me about dad,' Phoebe whispered.

Liz knew then that she must tell her daughter about her father, her time in Crete and the intense love that they had in the short time before Georgios had been taken from her. By the time Liz had finished her story, both mother and daughter were in tears, but both felt strengthened by the experience. Liz felt a burden had been lifted off her shoulders and Phoebe felt a small hole in her heart had been filled.

'Teach me the song, Mum. Please.' Phoebe pleaded.

In the hours that followed, Liz taught her daughter the melody she had written nearly 15 years before. When Phoebe played it, Liz could better appreciate the beauty of the song she had created and she felt a surge of love for her daughter and the man with whom she had made her.

Following that day, Phoebe would frequently talk about her father and Liz opened up about her feelings of love and loss. Sometimes Liz would hear Phoebe playing the song through her open bedroom door and she experienced a strange mix of pain and overwhelming affection at the musical thread that connected that moment to the past.

For her part, Phoebe added the song to her repertoire and if she felt nervous at a gig she would use it as a talisman to help her through. It always worked, and whenever she played the song it was loved by the people who came to watch her.

At school, reasonable passes in her GCSEs in English Literature and Drama coupled with a top grade pass in music enabled her to progress into the sixth form. She was relieved of the decision as to whether to go to university when she was spotted by an A&R man for a record label whilst playing on a bill in a local village hall. He promised her the earth, and her career in the music industry looked set to take off.

The summer when she would have taken her A Levels, Phoebe was playing on the same bill as some well-known artists to 'develop her talent', as the A&R man Steve said, before she was due to go into the studio the following year. In the months that followed she was hardly at home, travelling across the country from one venue to the next with barely a day off to rest. At first Phoebe felt a buzz of excitement at her tantalising proximity to fame but, as time went on, she felt the loneliness of being on the road away from her mother and the exhaustion of performing night after night.

She told herself that it was only for a short time until she got into the studio, then the touring would stop. As the months went by there was still no news of when she would make her debut record.

Then she heard from Steve that the record label had been bought out by another company, so things would be delayed; she just needed to be patient. At least then the touring stopped while she waited to hear how her career was to be progressed. In the end, it turned out that Steve was not part of the new label's plans and, so it seemed, neither was Phoebe.

When she heard the news, Phoebe was not as disappointed as she thought she would be. For a few months she relished staying home with her mother and grandparents but the ambition to perform never left her. To give herself an income she managed to find some session work and got in touch with some small local venues to try and get some bookings to perform.

Living in her grandparents' home, she didn't need much money and spent more and more of her time writing songs and less time trying to get gigs and, in the end, she would only perform when approached to do so. The edge was further taken off her ambition when she met Chris, a journalist on the local paper, on a night out at a pub in Salisbury with friends. Chris had gone to the same school as Phoebe but had been three years above her so their paths had hardly crossed. He was handsome, clever, confident and kind and it was not long before they became a couple and within a year they were engaged.

Phoebe was walked down the aisle by her mother who was brimming with pride as she gave her daughter away to her new son-in-law. For 25 years she had sacrificed everything to give her daughter the best she could. For a moment she shed a tear, thinking that the thread that had attached her to Georgios had at last been cut. Then she reminded herself that he lived on through her daughter and that line would continue through her grandchildren.

On her wedding night, Chris broke the news to his new wife that he had been offered a job at the BBC in London. She could tell he was thrilled and she was excited by the prospect of a new life in the city. Newly wed, she pushed aside the worry about moving away from her family and threw herself wholeheartedly into supporting her husband's ambition.

Following a short honeymoon in a rented cottage in Cornwall, the couple would take the long commute from Salisbury to London, where Chris began his new job while Phoebe visited estate agents searching for an affordable flat for them to rent.

They settled on an apartment above a café in Finchley. It was small, but Chris assured her that soon they would be able to buy a place of their own. He was as good as his word, and in less than two years they found a Victorian terraced two-up two-down in Teddington, a short journey to Chris's work in central London. Phoebe busied herself stripping wallpaper and sanding woodwork in their house and the small amount of session work she had been doing dwindled away. The cottage was not far from Bushy Park, and often Phoebe would take a walk across it to Hampton Court. She loved seeing the deer which grazed there, but often would think about the limitless miles of open space she used to walk on Salisbury Plain with her mother and grandparents.

Chris was working harder and harder as he stridently made his way up the career ladder. He left for work early in the morning and often worked late into the evening. The news that her grandfather had died suddenly of a heart attack hit Phoebe hard. When two years later her mother phoned to tell her that her grandmother had died of a stroke, Phoebe fell into a deep well of depression. She felt guilty that she could not do more to console her mother but her own grief was so deep it consumed her whole being. As time went by, the grief she felt subsided, only to be replaced by a numbness that would not go away and Phoebe found herself feeling less and less fulfilled. It was Chris who suggested they start a family, and slowly the thought of having a baby gave Phoebe's life a new sense of hope. Just the idea of having a child filled the void she felt in her soul.

As the months went by Phoebe's hope turned to anxiety as she didn't become pregnant. After more than two years of trying the couple agreed to seek medical help. When all other avenues had been explored, they were referred for IVF. The failure to get pregnant after three cycles of the treatment took its toll on Phoebe and the marriage. Through the years of trying to conceive, Phoebe had let the little work she had dwindle to nothing and by the time she had accepted she would never have children she had lost the motivation to start working again.

She stayed in bed late into the morning and was asleep by the time Chris arrived home, often late at night. It came as no surprise to her when he said he was leaving; she had suspected he was having an affair but found it hard to muster the energy to care. It came as a relief when, phoning her mother to tell her they were separating, Liz suggested that Phoebe come home.

Sad for the breakdown of her daughter's marriage, Liz was pleased to have company in the family home she had inherited. But it broke Liz's heart to see how unhappy her daughter had become, how she lacked any enthusiasm for life and had no self-confidence. Through her fragile beauty Liz could still see in Phoebe the daughter she remembered from before she married. She was determined to rebuild her daughter's confidence and help her find happiness.

As the autumn winds gusted over the plain and the days grew shorter, Phoebe fell into the same pattern of getting up late and walking round the house in her dressing gown. Liz cajoled her daughter to join her walking the dog on the chalk downs. Over the weeks the landscape worked its magic, gently reminding Phoebe of the idyllic times of her childhood. In the evenings, Liz would sometimes play her guitar, and encouraged her daughter to join her.

Six months on from the separation, her divorce was finalised and slowly Phoebe felt herself reconnecting with the world. Talking with her mother she realised that Chris had always put his interests first, with little consideration for her career or happiness. Little by little her mother began to build her daughter's strength. She persuaded her that she was still beautiful and that in her early forties it was not too late to rebuild her career. Phoebe began to write songs again and even plucked up the courage to play a few open mic nights in local pubs after years of shying away from playing in public.

During the daytime, Phoebe managed to wrap herself up in her music and the comfort of her mother's company, but alone at night she would often feel the darkness of her depression descend. She knew there was an empty space inside her which had not been left by the end of her disastrous marriage. Increasingly Phoebe found herself asking her mother about her father and Crete all those years ago. The more they talked, the more she felt the need to find out more about that part of her being which lay undiscovered. She knew she could never meet her father but perhaps absorbing more

116

about the half of her heritage she had left unexplored she could make herself whole again.

It was Liz who suggested to Phoebe that she make the trip, but it was something that Phoebe herself had been considering for some time. At the very least a holiday would do her good and maybe discovering something about the Cretan half of her ancestry would lighten the darkness that often gripped her. The sun on her face and the imposing landscapes would allow her to take stock of life and make friends with herself again.

At first Phoebe was enthusiastic about the idea. A romantic ideal of walking through shaded olive groves by the sea was the stuff dreams were made of. But as the idea turned into a possibility, doubts began to creep in. She was nervous of taking the trip to Crete by herself. She asked her mother if she would join her, but Liz felt her daughter needed to be alone if she was to discover what she was looking for. Liz made the excuse that she could not return to the place Georgios had been killed and that she had been deported from, which was not wholly untrue.

Before Phoebe could change her mind, they went online and bought an outbound flight to Heraklion, leaving the following month, and a one-night stay for the day of her arrival in the capital city; after that she would go wherever chance might take her. Together mother and daughter went shopping for clothes, sun cream and other holiday necessities. They pored over guide-books and Liz tried to recollect the places she had visited all those years before.

Phoebe was excited about the trip and although sometimes she felt a twinge of anxiety about going alone, she often felt something pulling her towards the island that had engendered half of her being. She knew that despite her unease, she had to go.

The flight would leave London's Gatwick airport in the early hours of the morning and Liz offered to drive her to the airport. Phoebe was unable to sleep and had packed her luggage in the car long before the time they had agreed. Checking in, she felt a pang of nervousness as her precious guitar, which she had brought at her mother's insistence, disappeared on the luggage conveyor.

Liz could see Phoebe was anxious. With time to spare she suggested they have a hot drink before she passed through into the departure lounge. Liz brought the coffee to the table and putting the cups down, took a box from her pocket and pressed it into her daughter's hands. Phoebe could see the emotion in her mother's eyes.

'I want you to have this.' A tear ran down Liz's cheek. 'Your father gave it to me… the night they took him away.'

Through the mist of her own tears Phoebe opened the box. Snuggled in the cushioned green lining was a gold necklace. She stared at the pendant: two exquisite bees placing a single drop of golden honey into a comb. Her mother reached into the box for the necklace and put it around Phoebe's neck.

Drying her eyes, Phoebe drank her coffee, stood and hugged her mother tightly, then walked towards the security gate.

Chapter 9

TOUCHING A HAND to her chest, Phoebe felt the precious pendant nestling beneath her dress as she stared in wonder at the exquisite golden exhibit in front of her: two bees dropping honey into a comb, the same as the necklace her mother had given her. She read that it was thought to date from 1800 BC and had been excavated from the graveyard of the Minoan palace at Malia.

The museum was one on the list of places her mum had recommended she visit, but in honesty Phoebe would have avoided it had it not been for the heat, noise and dust of the capital assaulting her senses. The air-conditioned archaeological museum had come as a welcome escape from the intimidating streets outside that fuelled her anxiety.

The journey had played havoc with her emotions. Taking off from Gatwick, her palms sweated as she gripped the arm rests on the seat. She couldn't concentrate to read. In the warmth of the cabin she eventually succumbed to sleep. When she awoke, the view below restored her equilibrium. Small islands floated on an expanse of sea, as tiny boats wrote signatures in white across the ultramarine velour.

The drive from the airport into Heraklion had seen Phoebe's disquiet resurface and she decided to leave her hire car in the harbour car park rather than brave driving the city streets. She walked along the harbour-front past the caiques and pleasure boats moored in the protective shadow of the Venetian fort which stood sentinel at the end of the sea wall. It felt strange to have her guitar case strapped over her back after all these years, but the memories it rekindled of her younger days were faintly reassuring. Phoebe headed uphill past shipping agents, banks, souvenir shops and waiters trying to coax her to eat in their tavernas.

She stopped beside a fountain topped by lions spouting water from their mouths. Sitting on the stone wall of the pool decorated with dolphins and nymphs, she reached into her bag and pulled out the directions to the hotel. She found it easily in a narrow side street nearby. Checking in, she showered before heading back out to explore. On another occasion Phoebe might have revelled in the warmth of the spring sunshine and the sounds and smells of the capital, but the events of the last few months had left her emotions raw. The crowds and traffic fuelled her growing claustrophobia and stumbling upon the museum she found a welcome refuge.

Inside, the cool was a relief as she wandered through the rooms displaying the Minoan collection. The alluring pendant had brought her up short. Seeing the real thing, she considered her necklace in a new light. She marvelled at the artistry of the jeweller who had applied the tiny beads of gold to the honeycomb and rendered the bees' curved bodies and outstretched wings. It was hard to imagine how something so small could be so bewitching.

Strangely, it gave her hope that there was a reason for this journey. It was tentative, but the way she had felt recently she was grateful for anything she could cling to. The breakup of her marriage had brought to the surface deep-rooted feelings she had not realised existed within her, as though something was missing and she was only part of what she was meant to be.

But she was beginning to realise that the hollowness she felt was not only about children, her divorce or lost career. It was about having never known her father and having no knowledge of the nationality which made up half of herself.

Now turning her head, Phoebe caught a glimpse of her reflection in the glass of the display cabinet. She had healed enough to have grown to like her face, its fragile beauty framed by her shoulder length blonde hair. She took a step backwards to avoid the look of the deep blue eyes staring back at her. What could they see? A forty-one-year-old woman, slim, a bit pale maybe, but someone with whom at moments she felt at peace. In the months following the separation, her mother had told her she was beautiful. If she didn't yet share that view, she had come far enough at least to be contented living with herself.

Phoebe turned her gaze back to the exquisite bees and reached for her own necklace, pulling it out from beneath her dress. As she walked through the airy halls of the museum taking in the incredible Minoan exhibits, she felt the tug of an invisible thread that connected her with those first Europeans. She had come to the island with no plan other than to escape the pall of depression that at times overwhelmed her in the country of her birth. Maybe by visiting the land of her unknown father she could fill in the cracks that had opened up in her being and make herself whole again.

Almost in a trance she wandered around, marvelling at the figures of a bull leaper, a snake goddess and a vibrant dolphin fresco all excavated from the palace of Knossos to the north of the city. But it was to the tiny bee pendant that she kept returning. Her mother had shared memories of the brief time she had spent with her father on the island. Maybe discovering the lost fragments of her own life would help Phoebe find her place in the world.

Mother and daughter had spent hours discussing where Phoebe might visit. She had decided to book a hotel for just one night in Heraklion, and then travel wherever serendipity might take her. She already knew that the city was not the place for her but maybe the pendant was leading her elsewhere. She remembered her mum talking about Malia, how she had stopped there and from the balcony of her pension had been able to reach out and pick oranges from trees in a grove which ran all the way to the sea. The way her mother had described the small seaside village, it sounded idyllic. With no other plans in place, why not follow the bees to the place that had been their home? It was somewhere at least to begin her journey. Phoebe found a space on a bench and took a map from her bag. Malia was not too far away, less than an hour's drive along the island's north coast. The site of the palace was to the east of the town.

Now she had a plan, Phoebe headed out onto the city streets. She knew she should have been hungry, but somehow in the heat she didn't feel motivated to eat. Suddenly her early-morning start caught up with her and she wanted nothing more than to sleep. Retracing her steps to the hotel and letting herself into the room, she closed the shutters and collapsed on the bed. She didn't emerge until dawn when the noises of the awakening capital stirred her from her slumbers.

After a breakfast of yoghurt and honey she checked out. Finding her car in the space she had left it at the harbour, she hesitantly drove through the busy streets from the port until she reached the national highway. She breathed a sigh of relief as she pulled out onto the main carriageway heading in the direction of the airport. Even at her cautious speed in the inside lane she was eating up the kilometres and in what seemed like no time at all she saw signs for Malia and turned off. She was excited to see this beautiful small village by the sea which her mother had told her about.

The picture Phoebe had in her mind from her mother's description in no way resembled the place she now encountered. Quad bikes weaved around double parked cars and coaches disgorged holidaymakers while groups of young men and women, some appearing drunk even at that early hour, fell in and out of the numerous fast food joints which lined the main street. Where she had imagined the groves of fruit trees were now block after block of holiday apartments.

Gripping the steering wheel tightly, it took all Phoebe's concentration to navigate her way through the town. One thing was certain; she would not be looking for a room for the night in Malia. Leaving the mayhem behind her, the road cleared as the sea of concrete gave way to flimsy greenhouses. Through torn plastic sheeting Phoebe could make out bunches of bananas growing inside. As the landscape opened up and the straight road crossed the coastal plain she began to relax, and she was pleased to see a sign for the archaeological site.

In the dusty car park, a hot breath of wind blew down from the mountains inland. Phoebe could hear the nearby waves breaking on the beach just to the north of where this arid shelf of land perched. She was amazed how quiet it was at the palace which had revealed so many treasures. The site had been rediscovered in 1915 and excavations were still going on to uncover the Minoan palace, town and graveyard which were destroyed around 1450 BC. Certain areas had been roofed over for protection but most of the ruins lay spread out in front of her eyes. In her guide book, Phoebe read how opinions differed about what brought about the demise of the palace, whether it was the same volcanic eruption which had overwhelmed Santorini and the likely tsunami that ensued, or whether it was razed to the ground by Mycenaean invaders.

Sauntering around, she crossed walkways over the more sensitive areas. Staircases which once ascended to second storey rooms now led nowhere but dazzling sapphire sky. The silence lent an added melancholy to the palace and Phoebe pondered how this served as a reminder of the fragile nature of even the most sophisticated of manmade conceits. Looking down, she could see the imprint of a lost society: an altar where sacrifices to the gods had been made, grain stores and giant pithoi which once held oil and wine.

Phoebe wondered at how a place of such archaeological significance and so close to Malia could remain deserted. She found herself walking out of the ruins, taking a path north towards the sea. She let the whispering of the waves guide her, but there was something else pulling her in that direction.

She felt an irresistible need to see the spot where the bee pendant had been taken from the earth. Less than a 10-minute walk away, in open ground not far from the sea, she came across the ancient cemetery of Chryssolakkos. Inside the grey limestone walls, the necropolis was divided into small rectangular plots which had been used as graves for the wealthy residents of the palace.

The guide book told her that the cemetery was given its name, meaning 'pit of gold', by local farmers who had unearthed a wealth of valuable artefacts as they tilled the earth. Of the golden jewellery which had been dug up from the graves, the bee pendant was the most celebrated.

Apart from the hiss of the nearby waves as they caressed the shoreline, the silence was profound. Phoebe let her imagination wander back into the past as her thoughts made a link with those

127

people who had lived on this spot in Minoan times. As she stood there on the barren plain by the sea, the spring sunshine bathing her in warmth, she felt those worries which had taken over her life for so many years drain from her. For the first time in so long she could see a future.

Standing there staring out at the vast expanse of sea somehow gave her perspective to look back on a time before those cares had begun to overwhelm her, when she had felt alive inside. A desire to play her guitar came over her, something she had done so little in recent years. She had only brought the instrument on her mother's insistence. Had her mum's intuition been prescient, had she a better understanding of how music could help heal her broken daughter than Phoebe had herself?

For a moment Phoebe stood rooted to the spot, afraid that the moment of wellbeing might be lost if she moved. She took a step towards the palace, gaining confidence as she began to walk. But where would she go? She knew one thing; she did not want to return to Malia.

Getting into the driver's seat, she longingly eyed the guitar case on the back seat before reaching into her bag for a map. She had still not thought about where she was going to spend the night. Reluctant to return the way she had already come, she scanned the way east instead. Where the north coast of the island sharply dropped away southwards she recognised a name her mother had spoken of: Spinalonga.

She remembered her mother had told her that this was the island that used to be a leper colony and that during her time on Crete she had visited it, and the island had had a profound effect on her. At the time, Phoebe had thought that going to see a place steeped in such a sad history might be morbid. But had she not just felt liberated by her visit to the cemetery of Chryssolakkos? She didn't have another plan. She would head in that direction.

For a moment she contemplated getting her guitar from the case and playing, but although there were no people around, she felt self-conscious. She decided her wish to play could wait to be satisfied until she found somewhere to stay where she could play in privacy. The early start and the walk in the open air had given her an appetite. In the short time she had been on Crete she had noticed there was no shortage of tavernas but she had in her mind's eye a picture of sitting outside eating a meal right on the waterfront. A place where she could plan and dream, give herself the time to relax and savour the wellbeing the pendant had bequeathed her. She ran her finger along the nearby coastline, coming to rest on the words Paralia Milatos written in tiny letters. It didn't look too far.

Finding her destination was not as simple as it had appeared, thought Phoebe more than half-an-hour later. Several times she missed turnings and had to retrace her way as signposts were hidden behind roadside bushes or were simply non-existent. Despite this she was enjoying her drive along the narrow tracks that wove through olive groves dotted with the occasional villa. Irrigation pipes snaked alongside the dust road which bucked across the undulating landscape. Above her on a hillside a pantiled chapel stood, its roof topped with a solitary bell hung from its arched belfry. In the background, the blue of the sea was so deep it denied any attempt to define it.

Phoebe pushed hard on the brakes as she nearly missed her way again, just stopping in time to follow a small sign to the beach. At the end of the road the sea spread out in front of her, calm, blue and boundless. She pulled in beneath the shade of a tamarisk tree beside rocks which fringed the waters beyond. Two cats lay on the boulders, lazily trailing their paws in rock pools. Next to where she had come to a halt was the restaurant she had imagined. Right on the waterfront, a covered terrace was served by the glass-fronted taverna opposite. As she got out of the car she could smell fish grilling on the coals of the outdoor barbecue tended by an elderly woman dressed in black.

A waiter gave her a table right beside the rocks and she ordered a cold beer while she studied the menu. Apart from three old men drinking coffee the taverna was empty. Feeling the warmth of the sun on her face, Phoebe was amazed that two of the men were wearing jackets, the other a pullover. Her mouth watered as she read the menu and she had to restrain herself from ordering what she knew would be too much food. In the end she decided on anchovies marinated in oil, a salad, grilled mackerel and chips.

Finishing her beer she asked for a small carafe of white wine to go with her meal. The chill of the red metal jug thrilled as she poured her drink into a tumbler. She took a sip: it was cold and dry. Glancing across the road she saw the waiter give her order to the woman at the outdoor grill and caught the enticing smell of the mackerel as they were put over the coals. She turned her head back seawards; the silhouette of a ship grew smaller as it ploughed a furrow towards Athens some 200 miles to the north. For a moment Phoebe closed her eyes and let the sun and the silence embrace her. It had been some time since she had felt so at peace with the world.

The waiter brought her plate of anchovies, some bread and a salad of tomatoes, cucumber and onion jewelled with clumps of feta cheese glistening in olive oil.

'*Kali orexi*, enjoy your meal,' he smiled.

Hungrily tearing off a chunk of bread, Phoebe wiped it in some oil before taking a mouthful of the salty anchovies. Looking down at the paper table covering, she saw it was a map of the island. Unlike the previous day when she had felt daunted by its

131

unfamiliarity, at that moment she felt excited by the possibilities it offered. She saw the island of Spinalonga, a small dot above a larger island off the coast of Elounda. The map had no roads marked so she lay her own on the table and plotted a route. Between where she sat and her destination was a headland through which passed no main-roads. She would need to go back inland onto the national highway towards the town of Agios Nikolaos before heading along the coast to Elounda.

She felt she could eat no more when the tiger-skinned mackerel arrived, crisp and lustrous, but Phoebe managed to devour them all and the plate of grapes and melon which followed. The waiter brought a small carafe of clear liquid to the table with the bill, along with two glasses; gesturing with his arm, he asked, 'May I?'

'Please, sit.'

'You like raki?' The waiter put the two small tumblers on the table, and without waiting for an answer he poured two glasses. '*Yamas*. Cheers as you say.' He lifted his glass and downed it in one.

'Cheers. *Yamas*.' Phoebe hesitatingly tried both her first word of Greek and taste of the fiery spirit. She felt the raw alcohol burn her throat before it warmed her stomach. Acutely aware that she had to drive, Phoebe held a hand over her glass as the waiter made to pour her another measure.

'It is good for you, it helps the digestion.'

Phoebe laughed but was not to be swayed.

'Where are you staying?'

'I'm hoping to visit Spinalonga, so am looking for somewhere near there, maybe Elounda?'

'You will like it,' said the waiter, smiling. 'It is not so far and very beautiful.'

He told her the story of the 'Island of Tears' and how it had become a more popular tourist destination since English author Victoria Hislop had written a bestselling novel about it 10 years earlier. He described a canal which had been cut through from the bay to Mirabello, and the ancient city of Olous which sank beneath the waves sometime in the eighth century, the salt flats, windmills, tiny hillside villages and more...

As he talked about Elounda and the leper island, Phoebe was convinced she had made the right decision. Her head was spinning with anticipation. She was eager to get there and find somewhere to stay. Making her excuses, she paid the bill.

Despite being parked in the shade of the leaning tamarisk tree the car seat was still hot, burning her bare legs, and she had to turn on the air conditioning and wait some minutes before the steering wheel was cool enough for her to hold.

Following signs for Agios Nikolaos, almost immediately she noticed a change in the landscape. The road began to climb through a steep gorge topped by the tower of a monastery peeping through a lush forest. On the other side of the hill the road continued into a tunnel through the mountains then past the ancient town of Neapoli. Villages nestled among the olive groves on the hillsides and Phoebe glimpsed dilapidated windmills among the orchards of almond trees.

On the edge of Agios Nikolaos she turned off, the road skirting the coast. As it climbed, in her rear view mirror she could see the splendour of the bay of Mirabello behind her. She pulled the car over at a viewing point half way up the mountainside and contemplated the sparkling gem of the town scrubbed and gleaming white, tucked into the corner of the huge bay.

If that view had made her heart leap, what awaited her as she drove over the summit of the hill at Lenika took her breath away. Beneath lay the bay of Korfos. She could see the canal which linked it with Mirabello and the bridge joining the causeway to the island of Kalydon, and the salt flats beside which lay the sunken city of Olous. In the distance she could just make out what she thought must be the small island of Spinalonga. She sensed some jeopardy as the road dropped steeply down the mountain towards Elounda and she struggled to keep her eyes off the amazing vista. Slowing to a safe speed, a taxi followed by a motorbike sped past, narrowly missing a coach climbing the hill in the opposite direction.

Finally she was in the small town itself, the road threading through tavernas, shops and houses before it opened out into a square beside the harbour, which also served as a car park. Seeing someone reversing out of a space she parked up, got out of the car and stretched her legs. *This will do nicely*, she thought, taking a seat in one of the cafés which looked out across the waterfront, *I will like it here*. Ordering a milkshake, she pondered where she should start looking for somewhere to stay. She liked the buzz of the square, but was drawn towards the causeway she had seen from the top of the mountain. She decided to start her search for a room from there.

Retracing her steps she drove out of the heart of the town, before taking a steep, narrow road which dropped down to the causeway heading towards the canal. On her right were many small hotels and apartments facing the water before giving way to the ancient salt flats which occupied the inland side of the spit. To Phoebe it felt as though the road was floating between them and the bay. A heron stood motionless on a rock in the enclosed beds. She

135

drove past a tumbledown building on the beach and headed for a stone bridge which connected the causeway with the island of Kalydon.

The cobbles shook her as she crossed over the canal and cautiously navigated the potholes in the unmade road passing two disused windmills, serene and sail-less. A breeze from the north tousled the bay of Korfos but to the other side of the canal, Mirabello shone like a looking glass polished to within an inch of its life. It was beneath these waters that Phoebe imagined the lost city of Olous lay.

On the canal were moored a few small caiques and some pleasure boats, their owners enjoying a late, lazy lunch in the waterfront taverna. There was only one other building that Phoebe could see, and she drove towards it along the track which teetered on the edge of the bay.

A large gate opened onto a driveway surrounded by a garden where urns were bursting with blooms of every colour. Getting out of the car she looked around her. It was perfect. The face of a woman popped up from behind the bar in the café which stood at the entrance to the villas.

'Welcome, how can I help you?' she asked.

Phoebe could not believe her luck when she was told there was a small villa available to rent. The woman led her through the pretty terrace café to a small traditional-style house with a balcony overlooking the gardens and out to the bay.

Returning to the car, she unloaded her bag and picked up her guitar case.

'You are a musician?' The young woman who had shown her the villa enquired, smiling.

Phoebe blushed. 'Well, yes I am. I mean, I was.'

'You do not stop being an artist. It holds you for life. Leave your guitar here. I will help you with your bag. Then you must sit, have a welcome drink and play.'

'Thank you.' Phoebe did not know what to say, the soft voice and twinkling eyes made her at ease with her host as she was led to the villa. Wasn't this what she had wanted to do as she stood beside the palace graveyard in Malia? She nervously followed the young woman back to the terrace café where she was shown a seat. The woman brought a jug of wine and two glasses to the table and sat. Unclicking the catches on her guitar case Phoebe lifted out the instrument. The café was empty, the only sound cicadas rasping a rhythmic accompaniment to the afternoon heat. Phoebe drew her fingers across the strings.

Chapter 10

AS PHOEBE PLAYED, the music took on a life of its own. Even though performing in front of a woman she had met just minutes before, she felt no nervousness as her music mingled with the scent of the flowers which hung in the warm afternoon air. There was something about this place beside the bay which was enchanting. She felt a connection, a feeling of homecoming.

A fishing boat was approaching the canal which joined the waters of Korfos with the sweeping bay of Mirabello. A fisherman stood at the tiller and waved and the owner waved back, laughing.

'You play marvellously. I'm Stella by the way.'

'I'm Phoebe. What a perfect spot you have here.'

The woman's face opened into a smile. 'We are very lucky.'

Comfortable in each other's company, the two women sat talking as the afternoon drifted into evening. Phoebe told her new friend of her plan to visit the neighbouring island of Spinalonga and Stella suggested she go early in the day to avoid the crush of coach parties and the heat which would make her visit to the island less enjoyable.

As darkness fell, Phoebe was invited to join the family for dinner, served on an old wooden table in the garden. She was made welcome by Stella's parents and younger brother whose conversation was tirelessly translated for Phoebe by her new friend. It seemed like an age since she had sat beside the sea eating lunch in Paralia Milatos and Phoebe hungrily tucked into the aromatic lamb kleftiko that was spooned onto her plate. It was long after midnight before she excused herself and made her way to bed.

Phoebe rose early as she had promised herself she would and, despite only a few hours sleep, felt refreshed. As she walked through the café where she had played her guitar the day before, she could see Stella already at work watering the gardens. The bay was like mercury as Phoebe set off over the cobbled bridge to the causeway which would take her to Elounda. On the rocks an old man sat fishing, his motionless figure silhouetted against the backdrop of the glistening bay of Mirabello.

On the outskirts of Elounda, in the hotels and apartments lining the seafront, waiters wished her '*kalimera*' as they busied themselves preparing for the day's business. When she reached the quayside she bought a ticket for the first boat leaving for Spinalonga, and had time to grab a coffee at a café on the square before the boat departed.

As she boarded the vessel she was joined by other early risers keen as her to avoid the crowds and heat. With the boat cast off from the quay, the welcome breeze blew Phoebe's hair across her face as the caique drew a line of white foam on the ultramarine water. As they neared Spinalonga, Phoebe could see an imposing fortress looking down on the steep stone walls which surrounded the island. The caique was eased bow first onto the end of a jetty and a gang plank put out for the passengers to disembark.

Paying her entrance fee, Phoebe was offered the chance of a guided tour. As it was early, the group was small and she joined an English guide who Phoebe hoped would help her understand more about the 'Island of Tears'. She was not disappointed. The story the guide wove of the history of Spinalonga was laced with sadness, hope and the familiarity of the everyday in an extraordinary situation. Phoebe found it difficult to reconcile thoughts of the tragic plight of the patients forced to live here with the way their day-to-day lives continued. She found it comforting to see the shops, taverna, hospital and church and to learn that many of the island's residents had got married and had children. But it was hard not to be affected by the poignancy of the struggles of the sick on such a sublime island.

The guide explained the bravery of the doctors who strove to find the cure which eventually ended the island's use as a leper colony. But Phoebe was angered to learn that despite the sickness now being treatable, in some countries the disease was still rampant. On the seaward side of the island, it was impossible not to be moved by the cliff top graveyard which had become so many of the islanders' final resting place.

Phoebe stared out to sea at the same view her mother had told her about when she had confided in her daughter about her first kiss with Georgios. The group had walked on ahead and Phoebe followed, alone with her thoughts.

The first of the big tour boats from Agios Nikolaos was docking and Phoebe was relieved that she had got to Spinalonga early. As her boat pulled away from the quay, she found it hard to leave her thoughts of the island behind her. When the belfry and domed tower framed in palm trees hove into view, Phoebe could almost feel the heat of the engines of the coaches arriving on Elounda's waterfront.

On another day she might have felt attracted to the hurly-burly of the square but it did not fit her contemplative mood. Along the dusty seafront track she politely ignored the appeals of the street waiters to eat in their tavernas. As the path gave way to the causeway she felt a welcome zephyr on her cheeks as she stepped out towards the bridge. The road arced between the shimmering waters of the bay and the tranquil salt pans as though floating. A small beach was beginning to fill up with swimmers and sunbathers staking their claims to the umbrellas.

Her eye caught a glimpse of a sign partly obscured by bushes; hand-painted in bright colours, it joyously indicated a taverna nestling behind the salt flats. Drawn towards the building hiding in the trees, she found it surrounded by a garden in full bloom and a multitude of pots displaying flowers of every hue. The recently watered earth released its cooling comfort as the sails of a small windmill turned slowly in the breeze. The seats under the shade of the pergola were empty and Phoebe was afraid she was too early. Turning to leave, she heard a voice.

'Please sit. Welcome.' A smiling woman gestured around her at the empty tables. 'Anywhere you would like.'

Phoebe picked a table in the shade with a view across the salt pans to the bay and to her villa on the island nearby.

'Would you like to eat, or just a drink?'

Skimming the menu the decision was easy, her mouth watered at the thought of the dishes on offer.

'We have some specials on the board as well, all fresh today.'

'I'd like to eat, thank you.'

While she was pondering the menu, Phoebe ordered an orange juice and a bottle of water. She settled on a dish of mullet grilled and served with a lemon sauce, some chips and a Greek salad. Outside the door to the kitchen an elderly couple sat, the woman shelling peas as two young children played among the tables and chairs.

Having given her order, Phoebe lay back into her chair, enjoying the view and the warm sunshine on her face, the only sounds to interrupt her thoughts the jabber of the children playing and the rasping of cicadas in the surrounding trees. Closing her eyes, it occurred to her that slowly she might be rediscovering a contentment she thought long lost.

On the outer reaches of her thoughts, her mind detected a new sound. A low humming noise got louder and Phoebe opened her eyes, looking around for the source of the emerging undertones which had turned into a buzz. The elderly man got up from his chair with an alacrity which belied his years, shouting to the waitress and gesticulating towards the garden.

Following his pointed finger, Phoebe could see the origin of the frenzied buzzing; in a tree to the edge of the pergola hung a dark cluster seething with life. All the time new bees were joining, adding their voices to the clamour of their swarm. Hearing the commotion, a young man in chef's whites emerged from the kitchen and after a heated discussion made a call on his mobile phone.

The noise from the swarm dropped to a background hum and the family became less agitated. Instead of returning to the kitchen the chef joined the elderly couple and the waitress sitting at the table to discuss the unwanted guests at their taverna.

Phoebe realised that her meal might be delayed, but was content to let the event unfold in front of her. She tore off a piece of bread from the basket and poured olive oil and vinegar onto her plate before dipping it in the tasty dressing. She had no idea how the situation would be resolved, but the chef did not look as though he would return to his kitchen any time soon. Phoebe was patient, enjoying the drama she had stumbled across.

It was some time before events took a turn with the arrival of a truck in the dusty car park beside the taverna. As its driver got out he was greeted by shouts from the chef and the old man both pointing towards where the bees had swarmed. Unflustered, the new arrival smiled and leisurely went to the back of his vehicle, lifting out a wooden box, a sheet and some other paraphernalia before reaching in the cab for a white beekeeper's suit.

As far as Phoebe could make out, the man was about her own age, tall with strong shoulders and a sharp and muscular frame. Before he pulled the veil over his head she could tell he was handsome and she couldn't help but stare.

Walking calmly towards the tree, he lay the sheet down beneath the swarm and placed the box to one side. Phoebe saw his white teeth form a smile behind the mesh as the family shouted advice from a safe distance. He then sprayed the swarm with a liquid and shook the branch of the tree and the bees separated themselves from each other and fell onto the sheet before flying into the box. He patiently waited until every bee had entered before putting a lid on the temporary hive.

Taking off his veil, Phoebe could see that the glint in the beekeeper's deep brown eyes matched the warmth of his smile as he walked past her carrying the box.

'*Kalimera*. Good morning.' The beekeeper took in the slim, blond-haired woman, his eyes holding her deep blue stare for a moment before he headed to his truck.

'*Kalimera*,' Phoebe responded, watching him carefully load the improvised hive onto the back of his four-wheel drive.

Returning, the beekeeper sat down with the family and was brought a frappé by the waitress. The chef returned to the kitchen and soon after Phoebe's meal was delivered to her table. The skin on the fish was salty and crisp, the white flesh tender and succulent and the salad fresh. Glancing across the courtyard she noticed the beekeeper was now also tucking into a meal. Even though she was full up by the end, Phoebe managed to finish the plate of melon and grapes and the accompanying raki brought by the waiter before settling the bill and setting off on the short walk along the causeway to the villa.

A sea breeze blew in from the north towards the bridge, ruffling the surface of the bay and taking the edge off the heat of the afternoon sun. A kite surfer was taking advantage of the wind to display his acrobatic talents, twisting and turning in the air high above the waves. In the distance Phoebe could see the convoy of boats ferrying trippers to and from Spinalonga and on the mountainside sugar cube villages sparkled amongst the silver green olive groves.

Getting up from the table where she had been reading in the garden café, Stella greeted Phoebe with a kiss on both cheeks.

'How was your trip? Can I get you a drink? Sit here.' She signalled for Phoebe to join her.

'Good. Just a water, thank you.' Phoebe sat as Stella reached into a fridge to get a bottle before going behind the bar to make a coffee. Gazing through the shrubs and tamarisk trees, Phoebe could see a small pebble beach and a stone quay jutting out into the bay. Stella returned with her coffee, and the two new friends talked about Spinalonga, the young Greek woman answering Phoebe's many questions about the history of the island. Deep in conversation, neither of them saw the truck pull into the car park. It was only when the beekeeper shouted Stella's name that they noticed the man Phoebe had seen earlier approaching carrying two jars. As he got near, Phoebe couldn't help but grin.

'*Yasoo* Andreas. Hello. Have you brought my honey?'

'Hello again.' The beekeeper flashed a gleaming smile towards Phoebe.

'You two have met?' Stella lifted an enquiring eyebrow at Andreas.

'Not formally. Stavros at the taverna called me out to deal with a swarm of bees and this beautiful lady was having lunch there. As I was over this way I thought I'd drop your honey off rather than make another trip.'

Phoebe felt herself blush; although embarrassed by the compliment she felt a warm glow inside.

147

'I see you like bees too.' Looking up, Phoebe saw the man looking directly at the pendant which hung at her chest. Feeling her cheeks getting redder she turned away.

'Andreas this is Phoebe, Phoebe, Andreas,' Stella said, trying to save her new friend's blushes. 'Phoebe's a musician.'

Usually Phoebe would have felt diffident at such an endorsement but at this moment was grateful for the diversion it gave to her thoughts.

'Would you like to join us for a drink?' Stella took the honey from the table and put the jars behind the bar, returning with some money from the till and a cold beer from the fridge for Andreas.

'What will you do with the bees?' Phoebe asked Andreas.

'I'll take them up to where I keep my hives on Katharo Plateau, they will be fine there. It is the perfect spot for them to live and work.' As Andreas talked about the bees he kept and the honey they made she could make out the passion he felt for his work.

'I have twenty hives there already and the bees produce honey which people seem to like.' He turned to look at Stella who nodded in confirmation.

Animated, he described how he tended his hives and extracted the honey which he sold to customers across the island.

Andreas was undoubtedly handsome but there was something elemental in his fervour for his work which Phoebe found attractive. As he spoke, she found herself drawn to the stranger she had just met.

'You are a musician?' Andreas changed the subject.

Before Phoebe could answer, Stella jumped in. 'She plays the guitar and sings beautifully.'

'That's kind of you to say,' Phoebe responded, feeling flustered under the weight of flattery.

'Why don't you play for us now?' At Stella's request, Phoebe could feel the discomfort welling up inside of her but could think of no polite way to refuse her host.

'I'll go and get my guitar.' Phoebe stood and walked to her villa. Why did she feel so nervous about playing in front of Andreas? He was friendly and engaging, and if she was not mistaken, liked her a little. She looked in the mirror hanging above the table in her bedroom and pulled a comb through her hair, sprayed some perfume behind her ears and around her neck before picking up her guitar and returning to the café.

Phoebe bent her head down over the guitar and fiddled with the tuning keys. Head still bent, she strummed the opening chords of a song, repeating the phrase several times until she found enough composure to raise her head and sing. As she went under the spell of the music, she glimpsed the widening smile and burnished eyes of Andreas as he settled into the back of his chair.

Coming to the end of one song she segued into another, not leaving space for a reaction from her audience of two. She warmed to their 'bravos' and excited claps but resisted leaving gaps in her performance where any self-doubt might infiltrate. Through the trees and across the bay she could see the distant peaks of the mountains. She dropped her gaze and her eyes caught Andreas'. A tear dropped onto the guitar and Phoebe realised she was crying. As the tears fell she continued to play until Stella wrapped a comforting arm around her and Andreas lifted the guitar from her grasp.

'I think we need a drink.' Andreas let himself behind the bar and poured a jug of wine from a barrel. Phoebe was sniffing and drying her eyes on a serviette, apologising to Stella. She did not know what had happened but in that moment of happiness she had realised the sadness that dwelled within her. As they drank, Phoebe started to open up to her companions in a way she rarely had, except with her mother. Even with Liz she had tried to avoid the subject of her father's death because she knew how much it would upset her.

The afternoon eased into evening while Phoebe poured out the story of her past. How the father she had never known had been a Cretan; how she couldn't have the children she yearned for; and how she had let slip the musical career she had loved and seen her marriage end in acrimony and divorce.

As she talked to these virtual strangers the weight of the past got lighter. Something about the land of her father made her feel more complete, and being able to play her music again in a spot so idyllic gave her hope for the future. There was something about her two new friends which she found comforting, their ability to live wholly in the present and find satisfaction in their day-to-day lives.

Andreas raised his glass from the table and stared deep into his wine. 'We have something in common. I never knew my father, or my mother.' Phoebe felt guilty when Andreas revealed that he had been adopted as a child.

'I'm so sorry. I have been talking about myself...' Phoebe nervously reached for the chain around her neck.

'Don't be sorry.' Andreas reached out and touched her arm. 'I had a happy childhood. Did you buy your necklace in Heraklion?'

'It was a gift from my mother; she gave it to me when I left her at the airport to come here. She told me my dad had given it to her.'

'I love it. Would you like it if I took you to see the real thing?'

'I've seen it, in the museum in Heraklion.' Phoebe answered, in an instant regretting that through her honesty she may have passed up the chance of going on a date with the engaging beekeeper.

'No, not the necklace. My bees. Katharo is in the mountains to the south of here, where I have my hut.'

'I'd love that!' Phoebe gushed, hoping she did not show her relief too obviously.

'In that case I will pick you up here in the morning at ten o'clock.' Looking at his watch, Andreas stood. 'I'm late, I must get off. I'll see you tomorrow.' His brown eyes held Phoebe's gaze for a moment before he headed towards his truck.

'I think you have an admirer,' said Stella. 'Andreas has been supplying us with honey for years and he has never offered to take me to see his hives in the mountains,' she laughed, 'or told me that he was an orphan.'

Stella went behind the bar, returning with the jug refilled with wine and a plate of flaky, honey filled pastries and some blood red water melon. Across the water the lights of Elounda twinkled like the stars which shone down on them from the clearest of night skies. Snatches of music blew in on the warm air across the bay as the two women sat chatting long into the night.

Chapter 11

PHOEBE EASED HERSELF out of bed and stepped onto the balcony. Not a breath of wind tousled the surface of the bay or stirred the leaves on the tamarisk trees. The hiss of the irrigation system made her start as it began to water the gardens below, the scent of the blossom a promise of all the new day had to offer.

Having left herself plenty of time to get ready, when Phoebe looked at her watch she realised she had spent longer than usual doing her hair and make-up and did not have time for breakfast. Grabbing her bag she shut the door behind her and made her way outside just as she saw Andreas' truck bumping over the bridge along the causeway.

Stepping down from the cab, the beekeeper gave Phoebe a kiss on both cheeks before holding out an arm to help her up into the passenger seat. She smelled a hint of aftershave and the strong arm she leant on reassured her that she had not been dreaming about the attractions of the man she had met the previous day.

It was already getting hot, and Phoebe reached in her bag for a tissue to wipe her forehead.

'It is going to be a warm day, but up in the mountains it will be much cooler. It will be perfect, I think.'

Andreas shot her a smile before swinging the truck through the gates. In the morning light the blue of the sea merging with the sky was tantalising. A caique puttered under the bridge through the canal, making its way to the wider reaches of the bay of Mirabello. The sail-less windmills looked on as a falcon dived into the scrubland beside the salt flats. Waiters hosed and brushed their terraces to within an inch of their lives, stopping to wave and shout to Andreas as they made their way along the waterfront.

Leaving Elounda, leaning out the window Phoebe could make out the island of Spinalonga in the bay and see her villa and the canal beneath her. As they reached the summit, the view down towards Agios Nikolaos was spectacular as a huge cruise ship was being cajoled by tugs onto an improbably small quayside.

When the road turned away from the sea, the landscape changed from the sublime to the mundane as they drove past factories, garages and industrial units before merging with the main highway which bypassed the town. The road rose again as they headed inland towards Kritsa, where Andreas told Phoebe he lived. He explained that it was Crete's largest village which had been perched at the head of this lush valley since Minoan times and was close to the remains of the ancient city of Lato. Phoebe could see the green swell of olive trees running down to the sea, while above her the peaks of the Dikti mountains towered over them. Andreas proudly told her how the town of Agios Nikolaos was originally a mere acolyte to Lato, the port which served this city in the hills.

Driving through the narrow flower-adorned streets, they passed elderly women in black mufti bent over their needlework, cats snoozing beneath their rushwork chairs. Phoebe would have liked to have stopped and explored the labyrinth of alleyways which squirreled their way towards the outer reaches of the village. Maybe another day she would visit Andreas' home.

She smiled at the thought as they left Kritsa behind. Above the village Andreas pulled off the road. Looking down on the cluster of houses he pointed out how it resembled a scorpion nestled on the hillside. She was not sure whether Andreas was joking when he said that planning regulations forbade people building outside the unique boundary of the village.

As they climbed, Phoebe could feel the air cooling, the groves of olives now dotted with cypress, maple and holm oak. Andreas slowed the truck to walking pace as they tagged along behind a herd of goats, their bells echoing through the hills, making their way to pastures new. Andreas told her how the fertile lands of Katharo were owned communally by the people of Kritsa. Here they could graze their goats and sheep, grow fruit and vegetables and keep their beehives; and those who made use of the land paid a part of their income back into the community.

During winter, he said, the land was inhospitable with no mains electricity or water. Snow regularly covered the ground, and access without a four-wheel drive vehicle was almost impossible. In the autumn the herds were driven down the mountain to their winter pastures on the lower ground surrounding the village. Any power had to be created by diesel generators and farmers filled water tanks from natural aquifers and hoisted them onto the roofs of their isolated farmsteads to supply their needs.

'Look!' Andreas pulled off the road, getting out of the truck and pointing skywards to a huge bird riding the thermals over the mountaintops. 'A Lammergeier vulture. It is looking for dead animals. When it sees one it will swoop down and pick up the bones and carry them high into the air and drop them to smash so it can eat the marrow.'

'What a view he must get from up there.' Looking around, Phoebe found it hard to imagine a panorama which could surpass what she was seeing herself. Down the mountain through the heat haze she could just make out the sea merging almost imperceptibly with the sky. Turning around, the plateau was bursting with wildflowers, a carpet of yellow dotted with red poppies, white daisies and purple campanulas.

'Sometimes I see a golden eagle, and there are quite a few griffon vultures too. Now I will take you to see the hippos and elephants and maybe a goat up a tree.'

'Now you are being silly.' Phoebe said, laughing, as she hoisted herself back into the truck.

Andreas pulled onto an unmade track and engaged four-wheel drive. Phoebe had to hold tight, afraid of bumping her head on the roof as the vehicle navigated the deep ruts and steep inclines, twisting and turning across a hillside dotted with apple and pear orchards, vineyards and arable land put over to the growing of cereals. Dropping down onto the plateau the landscape was sparser and the tinkling of bells grew louder. All around Phoebe could see goats grazing on the meagre spoils growing through the rust-coloured rocks.

'There!' Phoebe followed Andreas' pointed finger. High in a tree, balancing precariously, was a goat stripping a branch of its foliage.

Phoebe leaned in her bag for her camera, but the shy beast sought the camouflage of the leaves. 'Don't worry, you'll see plenty more.' Andreas was as good as his word. As they drove further into this wilderness on the top of the world, Phoebe spotted any number of subjects she could take snaps of.

'Now all you've got to do is find me the hippos and elephants you promised me.' Phoebe turned as Andreas took his eye off the track and smiled. 'Look where you're going!' she shrieked, punching his arm.

'Don't you trust me? You will just have to be patient.'

Pulling back onto a made road, Andreas found his way to an isolated cluster of dwellings and a couple of tavernas. With the engine turned off, the cool air was silent and carried on it the smell of mountain thyme.

'Would you like something to eat?' Andreas asked, jumping from the truck and opening the passenger door for Phoebe.

She followed Andreas into a taverna. From the dark of the inner room a man and woman appeared, enthusiastically greeting Andreas before shaking Phoebe's hand. Almost immediately a welcome drink of raki was brought and Andreas ordered for them both. The man disappeared into the dark of the kitchen, and within minutes appeared with two plates of potato omelette and a salad

158

bursting with juicy tomatoes, plump olives and salty, crumbly feta, accompanied by a plate of dried rusks.

While they ate, Andreas translated as the owner proudly explained that everything he served was produce from the surrounding plateau, and Phoebe had to agree that the delicious meal she was eating was just perfect in its simplicity.

'Now I must show you the hippos and elephants,' said Andreas, a sparkle in his eye. Turning to the owner, he spoke some words in Greek before crossing the terrace and picking up a battered suitcase which lay on a table in the corner and returning with it to where they sat.

Flicking the catches, he opened the case. Phoebe half rose from her chair to peer inside. One by one Andreas lifted out a selection of bones. To her amazement Phoebe learned that these were the remains of dwarf hippopotamus and elephants which roamed the island during the mid-Pleistocene period. Incredulous, she was not sure this was not a joke until Andreas showed her printed information in English from the Natural History Museum in Heraklion confirming the story.

Found nearby, the bones were evidence of how these unlikely creatures once inhabited the plateau. Andreas said it was thought they might have got there on ice floes during the Ice Age of 540,000 years ago. Originally full-sized, the species evolved to be smaller as food supplies dwindled. Eventually having to compete for food with more nimble species they became extinct during another Ice Age about 100,000 years ago.

Something about being able to touch these bones of animals which lived so long ago Phoebe found moving. What was it about this island that constantly made the links between past and present so strong, so immediate? Andreas went to his truck and returned with a large jar of honey which he gave to the owner. His attempts to pay for lunch were waved away, his friend almost offended that he should even ask.

They returned to his truck and, heading off road again, the sense of isolation was enthralling and Phoebe was astonished whenever they met another vehicle sharing this wilderness. Every now and then Andreas would stop and leap out, returning with a flower, or a herb for her to identify, or to point out lizards sunning themselves on rocks and birds hovering high above. He was passionate about everything in the environment and Phoebe felt delight in sharing this place he loved with him.

Andreas turned the truck off the track, and she gripped the dashboard as the vehicle pitched down a steep path. Emerging into a glade, Phoebe could see the brightly painted hives nestling beneath the surrounding trees and could hear the sound of running water from a stream somewhere in the nearby hills. In one corner of the clearing, a small white concrete structure was the only blemish on this otherwise idyllic spot.

'Do you like my hut?'

'It's lovely.' Phoebe said, reserving judgement on the stained, single-windowed cube topped with a large black plastic water tank.

Inside, the hut belied its uninviting exterior. The white-painted walls were clean, and multi-coloured woven rugs covered the concrete floor. In one corner was a cast iron stove and against a wall was a wooden bed draped in a woollen blanket. On the opposite wall was a worktop with a camping stove and a few glasses, cups, pots and pans and shelves of jars and candles. Off the main room was a tiny washroom and toilet. Outside, a wooden lean-to housed Andreas' centrifuge and other apiary equipment and beside the door was stacked a pile of logs.

'It's got everything I need for when I stay up here,' Andreas said proudly.

'It's lovely,' Phoebe repeated, this time meaning it.

'Shall we go outside and see the bees?'

Phoebe blinked as Andreas led her back out into the afternoon sunlight. He went to his truck and pulled his beekeeper's suit and two veils from the back.

'If you want to see the bees you'd best put this on.'

161

The suit was far too big for Phoebe and Andreas stooped to roll up the legs before turning up the sleeves and handing her a pair of oversized gloves before putting on a veil himself. 'They are usually very calm, it is unusual to get stung but I think you will feel safer with the suit on.'

Phoebe noticed that Andreas did not wear gloves. Taking what looked like a tin with a cone on the top and small bellows attached to the side Andreas opened up the device and put a handful of fuel inside before taking a lighter from his pocket and setting fire to it. Replacing the lid he tested the bellows and smoke poured from the spout.

'Aren't you going to wear gloves?' Phoebe asked.

'They know me well, and the smoker will keep them quiet for a while.'

As they approached a bright yellow hive, Phoebe could hear the low buzzing of the bees. Taking off the top, Andreas blew smoke inside before removing a frame and puffing more smoke over its surface. Through her veil Phoebe could see the hexagonal cells capped with beeswax, inside which the golden product of the bees' labours was housed.

'Shall we harvest some honey?' Removing two more frames, Andreas put the lid back on the hive, and carried them to the lean-to.

Taking a knife from his pocket, he scraped the wax into a bucket before tipping it into a cloth which he suspended over a plastic bowl, explaining that more honey would drain out overnight and then the valuable wax could be used for making candles or soap. He then slotted the uncapped frames into a hand-cranked centrifuge. 'Would you like to turn it?' Phoebe wound the handle and felt the frame begin to spin.

Whilst she turned the crank, Andreas disappeared inside, coming back with a jar. Checking the frames, he opened a tap at the bottom of the extractor and the golden liquid poured into the pot he held beneath.

'Have a taste.' Andreas held the jar towards Phoebe. Taking off the veil, she dipped a finger in the sweet, smooth honey, licking it before it ran down her hands.

'Do I still need to wear the suit?' Phoebe laughed.

'I think it will be quite safe to take it off now. Let me get you something to wipe your hands first.'

From the hut Andreas returned with a damp cloth and washed Phoebe's hands. Undoing the front of the bee suit, she struggled to get the elasticated trousers over her shoes, stumbling. Andreas caught her and as she turned her head to thank him she knew in that moment she wanted him to kiss her. Something in her eyes communicated her longing to Andreas, who pulled her to him.

Andreas pulled the suit down over her shoulders, before bending down to support her as he gently tugged it over her shoes. Phoebe quivered slightly as the air cooled her skin and noticed the sun beginning its descent towards the mountaintops.

'Shall we stay and watch the sunset?' Phoebe wanted nothing more.

'Yes, I'd like that.'

Andreas brought two blankets from inside the hut. One he spread on the floor the other he wrapped around Phoebe's shoulders before returning for a jug of wine. As they sat watching the sun go down, Phoebe rested her head on Andreas' chest and sensed a belonging she had not felt for a long time.

When the sun had set and the chill of the mountain night engulfed them, Andreas lit some candles and took wood from the log pile to set a fire in the stove. From a barrel in the kitchen he poured more wine and from a cupboard took dried rusks, olive oil and a hunk of hard cheese before disappearing to harvest some tomatoes from his vegetable patch.

The simple food tasted like a banquet, and in what remained unsaid between them lay agreement that they would spend the night together.

Chapter 12

PHOEBE AWOKE ALONE. It took a moment for her to take in the unfamiliar surroundings. She warmed as memories of the night before permeated her early morning thoughts. Wrapping a sheet around her she stood and looked out of the window. The grass shone with a moist glow as the last vestiges of the dawn haze rose above the trees. On the other side of the clearing Phoebe could make out Andreas tending his hives.

Standing by the window, she watched him for several minutes as he carefully removed frames, bending to check on the welfare of the bees before gently sliding them back into their homes. Totally consumed by his early morning task, there was something about Andreas' preoccupation with his work which rooted him in this enchanted spot and connected him with a heritage which went back thousands of years to Minoan times. Phoebe reached for the pendant around her neck and wondered at the joy she had found at this stage in her life.

Leaving the hut she crossed the clearing, the last trace of dew caressing her legs as she walked through the grasses and wild flowers. The bright colours of the hives, red, yellow and blue, further cheered her already elated mood. Just as she came upon him Andreas raised his head, turned and kissed her. A lone bee from the hive settled on Phoebe's bare shoulder.

'See, he likes you.' Andreas held out a hand and the bee flew to him before being ushered into a hive.

'I'll make us some coffee.' Andreas moved towards his hut. 'If you have nothing better to do today we could visit the Lassithi Plateau? I need to drop some honey off at a taverna there, but apart from that I am free.'

Inside, Andreas put the briki on his camping stove, patiently waiting for the bubbles to rise to the top. Pouring the foam into two small cups he then divided the rest of the coffee, carrying the cups and two glasses of water to the small table outside.

Meanwhile, Phoebe washed as best she could under the trickle of cold water in the makeshift shower, towelled and tied back her hair, dressed and re-emerged into the sunlight.

166

As Andreas navigated the truck across the rugged mountain terrain around Katharo, his love for these isolated uplands shone through his words. He spoke to Phoebe of the neighbouring, much larger plateau toward which they were bumping their way, telling her how, until recently, it had been covered by thousands of windmills in full sail, drawing water to feed the fertile soil. These had been replaced in the name of progress by generators but there was now talk of these being switched for wind turbines as the cost of electricity was so expensive.

It was in the mountains that surrounded the plateau that Zeus was born, in the Diktean Cave near the village of Psychro. This was the place that the god's mother, Rhea, had fled to escape Kronos who, believing that one of his own children would depose him, had eaten their first five progeny. After giving birth to the king of gods, Rhea substituted the baby for a rock swaddled in clothes which, when Kronos caught up with her, she presented to him and he swallowed, whilst the baby Zeus was smuggled to the foothills of Crete's tallest peak, Mount Psiloritis. Kronos was right to be worried. When Zeus grew into adulthood he came after his father, making him disgorge his other siblings who then overthrew him and divided up the world into the kingdoms that each would preside over.

Reaching the crest of the hills that surrounded the plateau, Andreas brought the truck to a halt. Even without its windmills the view was breathtaking. It was like a lost world, ablaze with colour, a flat patchwork quilt of fertile land cradled between the mountain ranges of Dikti and Selena. Small villages were dotted around a road which traversed the highlands, marking out the circumference of this extraordinary land of plenty.

Dropping down onto the road they drove through fields sprouting with the first stirrings of crops and orchards in blossom, a pink and white canopy protecting the army of blood red poppies beneath. Andreas pointed out the occasional iron skeletons of rusting windmills, a forlorn reminder of the past, but thoughts of their demise did little to dampen Phoebe's excitement at what she was seeing.

A coach overtook them, speeding towards the Diktean Cave, Andreas raising his head and tutting as it overtook an elderly woman riding her laden donkey.

'I think we'll give the cave a miss today if you don't mind?' Andreas turned towards Phoebe. 'The legend is far better than the reality and it will be overcrowded with tourists. The place I am delivering my honey should be much more satisfying.'

Phoebe was content to let the day play out in whichever way Andreas chose. How right her mum had been to suggest she come to Crete to discover the land of her dead father. How lucky she had been that the pendant her mother had passed on to her had proved such a talismanic gift.

Following the road around the rim of the plateau Andreas stopped in the village of Tzermiado, at the base of Mount Selena. He parked beside a taverna on a street corner, the pavement on both sides covered with tables shaded by trees. No sooner was he out of the truck when he was greeted by the owner who was introduced to Phoebe. After Andreas had handed over his honey they were enjoined to sit.

'It's a bit early for lunch,' Andreas said to his friend. 'If you don't mind we'll take a walk and then come back to eat.'

Taking Phoebe by the hand, they walked to the edge of the village and then out along one of the paths which crossed the plateau. Andreas explained that the village was considered the capital of the region, and like other settlements was build on the edge of the plateau, leaving the flat, fertile soils free to farm. All around them spring had seen the first flourishing of the myriad of fruit and vegetable crops in fields divided by irrigation channels which criss-crossed the land. Content in each other's company, they walked between the fields before their route returned them to the village and the taverna.

'I hope you are hungry now?' Andreas asked as they took a table beneath a sunshade.

Phoebe was. No sooner had they sat down than a waiter brought them two beers, the glasses frosted with ice. The plates of hot and cold mezzes that followed could barely fit on the table and a waiter pulled up another to squeeze on more dishes. Cheese, fish, flaky filled pies, zucchini flowers, stuffed tomatoes, dolmades and salads just kept arriving. When they had finished, Phoebe could not believe how much they had eaten and was amazed at herself when she accepted the offer of a masticha ice cream, a speciality of the taverna which Andreas told her was made on the premises.

The owner brought raki, and Phoebe could hear herself opening up to Andreas about her past, her failed marriage and thwarted career. He proved a good listener, encouraging her to tell him about her life in England whilst remaining guarded about his own past. When he spoke, he talked about the island he loved, the mountains, the sea and the history of the people who had inhabited this mystical land since the beginning of time.

In the mountains above them, he told her, was the settlement to which the last Minoans had retreated. After the demise of Knossos and other cities around the island, it was thought that they had survived high up on the inhospitable outcrop of Karfi for 400 years, well into the Dorian period. From this lofty spot more than 1000 metres above the sea they could watch for approaching enemies.

'Would you like to walk up there, it will only take us a couple of hours.' It was only when Andreas smiled that Phoebe could see he was joking. She was not even sure she could walk as far as his parked truck. 'Or we could go back to the hut for a siesta?'

The second option felt much more appealing to Phoebe and she grinned in agreement.

*

Phoebe was woken by the ringing of a phone and felt Andreas relax his sleeping embrace to retrieve the mobile from his trousers which lay discarded somewhere on the floor of the hut. As he spoke she could hear the anxiety in his voice as he went outside to continue his conversation.

'I am sorry, something has come up and I need to get home.' Andreas said as he came back through the door. 'I will take you back to your villa first.'

Phoebe could sense the urgency in his voice and started pulling on her clothes whilst Andreas waited outside swinging the keys to his truck impatiently. He started the engine before Phoebe got into the vehicle, and as soon as she was seated he sped away from the clearing. As they drove along the mountain tracks, Phoebe held on for dear life and daren't disturb Andreas' concentration by talking.

How different his mood now was to the day before when he had brought her up to the plateau.

Phoebe's mind was full of concern at what had caused such a change in Andreas. Just moments earlier they had been sharing a bed together. Now he stared ahead, anxiety written across his face as he sped down the mountain roads. It took him half the time it had taken the previous day to make the journey. Swinging the car round in an arc he stopped in the car park at the villas and as soon as Phoebe had jumped down from the truck he sped away.

Watching Andreas drive away from the villas, Phoebe was left pondering his parting words, 'I will see you soon.' Little more than an hour earlier she had been lying in his arms feeling safe and secure. Now she felt unsure of where she stood in their relationship. Had she stupidly misread the signs? Would she see Andreas again, or had he seen her as just a short-term fling? She told herself that she was being stupid, that of course he would come back soon, but he didn't have her mobile number and she had no way to contact him.

She spent the rest of the afternoon and evening in her villa, not wanting to see anyone else. She tried to play her guitar and then to read but she found it impossible to concentrate. That night she found it hard to sleep. With her husband she had felt nothing when he left, but although she had only known Andreas a couple of days, she could not bear the thought of losing him. Her mind flitted between thoughts that the relationship was over and that she should be patient and wait for Andreas to return.

The following morning Phoebe had decided to let fate take its course; it had stood her in good stead so far. Nevertheless, she found herself spending the day at the villas, swimming on the beach, reading on her balcony and eating in the café. Although she tried to put Andreas out of her mind, in her heart of hearts she knew she was hoping he would return to see her.

Another sleepless night trying to come to terms with her feelings was too much for Phoebe. As a woman approaching middle age, she told herself how foolish she was to have fallen for any man who would desert her so easily, but something still pulled at her heart. Could she stand another day just waiting for something which might not happen? She had to take things into her own hands.

Phoebe thought she could remember the way to Kritsa. Surely if she went there she would be able to find the beekeeper's house. Retracing the route she had taken with Andreas, this time she hardly noticed the views which had so enchanted her a few days earlier. All her energies were taken up with remembering the way and with thoughts of how she would track him down.

She parked beside a small square and walked up the hill past a large church flying the blue-and-white flag of Greece and the yellow and black ensign of the orthodox religion, its twin-headed eagle crowned with a mitre flapping in the breeze.

As Phoebe walked along the main street between the shops selling traditional crafts and tourist tat, she began to see the scope of her task. The village was larger than she had first thought and a labyrinth of streets spread out in all directions. Everywhere she looked, white houses stepped up the mountainside along narrow roads lined with pots bursting with flowers. In the heat of the day walking up and down the steep paths was exhausting and it occurred to her that she would not know which of the houses Andreas' was anyway. It had been a stupid idea coming to look for him. A thought occurred to her, why had she not asked Stella for his phone number? Was it that she was embarrassed of her feelings for the beekeeper? Maybe she should go back to Elounda and wait patiently to see if he would return. If not, she would have to try and forget him.

Disconsolate, Phoebe made her way back to the main street, towards the square where she had left the car. She found herself window shopping, reluctant to act on her decision to give up the search. Peering into a shop selling herbs, oil, soaps and other gifts, she noticed a display of jars of honey. Instantly she recognised the

174

labels as being the same as on the jar she had filled with Andreas up on Katharo just days before. Maybe they held the clue to finding where her absent lover lived?

Picking up a jar, she scanned the label for an address. Tantalisingly the label held what she believed was the information she was looking for, but it was in Greek and Phoebe could not decipher it.

'This would make a very nice present.' The shopkeeper made Phoebe start. 'It is the best honey, made locally on a plateau above the village.'

'Thank you. I think I'll buy one.' Phoebe handed the jar to the woman in the shop.

'Is it a gift, I will wrap it for you?'

'Thank you. That would be perfect.' Phoebe said.

Walking back up the hill she waited until she was out of sight of the shopkeeper before she guiltily tore the wrapping from the jar of honey. Stopping at each tiny alleyway she compared the names to the one written on the label.

She saw Andreas before she could confirm the address on the jar. Coming out of a house, he was carrying a young boy and holding the hand of a younger girl. Shocked, Phoebe took a step back and peered around the corner up the alleyway. At that moment her worst fears were confirmed as a woman followed him out of the door, running her hand down his back as she waved him goodbye.

Distraught, Phoebe turned and ran down the main street. He must not see her. How had she been so stupid, trusting a man she knew so little about? She held back her emotions until she got into the car and then the floodgates opened. Through the tears she managed to make a U-turn before setting off. Above the bay a dark cloud hovered and by the time she had reached the outskirts of Agios Nikolaos large drops of rain were thumping on the windscreen. The storm was ferocious, and it took all Phoebe's strength of will to pull herself together as she climbed the hill towards Lenika. She could hardly see the way ahead and had to slow to a speed at which the car could barely make the climb. A river of water flowed downhill as she struggled towards the summit.

As quickly as the storm had started it ended. As she reached the top of the hill, the sun broke through a tear in the cloud revealing the gulf of Korfos. A rainbow arched overhead, dropping down into the sea somewhere behind Spinalonga, which sparkled like a rough diamond in the distance. Although she was relieved to be safe, the stunning panorama which would normally have brought a smile did nothing but sharpen Phoebe's focus on the events of the morning. Again the tears began to fall, rolling down her cheeks and dropping on her legs as she drove along the peninsula road towards the refuge of her villa.

She hoped to get to her accommodation unseen. The café was empty. Crossing the terrace she thought she had gone undetected when Stella appeared carrying a pile of sheets. Halfway through her greeting she stopped. Seeing Phoebe's distress, Stella deposited the linen on a table and wrapped her arms around her.

'You are crying. What is the matter? Please sit and have some water and we can talk. Maybe it will help?'

All Phoebe wanted was to be alone, but she did not want to be rude, and maybe opening up to Stella would do no harm. Sitting down and breathing deeply, she told her friend how after Andreas had not contacted her, she had gone in search of his home and what her search had revealed: that the man who had become her lover was married with children.

Stella's reaction was not what Phoebe would have expected. A momentary look of amazement was replaced by a smile as the Greek woman leaned forward across the table and hugged her.

'But Andreas is not married.'

Phoebe could not believe what she was hearing.

'So who were the woman and children I saw coming out of his house?'

'They are his kids, and she is his sister in law.'

Stella could see from the confusion on Phoebe's face that this news had not made things better. 'Andreas is a widower, poor guy. His wife died nearly three years ago. His sister-in-law helps him look after the kids. There is nothing between them.'

Phoebe's relief was tinged with sadness for Andreas and at how stupid she felt at jumping so hastily to conclusions. She should have known better than to try and track him down. Why had she not trusted him? Had he spotted her running away; and what would he think about her going to his home uninvited?

'Andreas took his wife's death very hard. All his friends worry about him. To the world he looks untroubled but deep down the tragedies in his life have taken their toll. When you didn't return to your villa the other night, I hoped that maybe he had been able to move on.' Stella stood and went to the bar, taking two bottles of water from the fridge, and sat down again before she continued. 'No harm has been done. He probably didn't notice you in Kritsa.'

'Thank you.' Phoebe unscrewed the lid from her water and took a mouthful. 'I don't know why I thought what I did.' Phoebe's voice dropped to a whisper.

'I'm not surprised. It must have been strange when he didn't take you to his house. I think it must be hard for Andreas to build a new life,' said Stella. 'He is very private, but I know one thing, he would not have let you get close if he was not very fond of you.

This is what he needs, but it may take him time to resolve his feelings.'

'It was stupid of me.' Phoebe suddenly felt full of remorse. 'All I was thinking of was myself. I never considered what was going on in his life... He should have told me though.'

Stella reached a hand across the table as she saw Phoebe succumb to her emotions. As the tears fell she didn't know whether it was through sadness or relief but she did know that she had never cared about a man so much before in her life.

'You haven't lost him,' Phoebe comforted her. 'You just have to let time take you both where it will. You weren't stupid to go and find him. Perhaps he could do with your support to find a way forward in his life; maybe he needs you to be the strong one?'

'Do you think I should go back to Kritsa and find him?'

'What harm can it do? If he is not pleased to see you, at least you will know where you stand. Be brave.'

Although Stella's response was what she wanted to hear, brave was not what Phoebe felt as she rinsed her face and sat to reapply her make-up. Looking in the mirror, she wondered what Andreas could possibly see in her. Her resolve faltered. Standing, she walked outside onto the balcony. From the garden below the earth smelt fresh after the recent storm and the bay shone like a looking glass as she stared across at the honey-coloured buildings of

Elounda tumbling down the distant hillside. This is my here and now, Phoebe thought. And it is sublime. With renewed determination she returned to the dressing table and finished fixing her face. Maybe it's not so bad after all, she reflected before standing and heading for the door.

An hour later, Phoebe stood in front of the door in Kritsa with knots in her stomach. The shutters on all the houses were closed along the sleepy alleyway. A rogue fig tree sprouted through a crack between the wall of a derelict house and the path. Either side of the door, pink and red geraniums cascaded from two large olive oil tins. The step up to the entrance was framed by a bougainvillea in full bloom, its blown purple petals covering the ground like confetti. Taking a deep breath, Phoebe grasped her courage and at the same time took hold of the cast iron knocker.

The door was opened by a beautiful dark-haired woman, whose deep brown eyes smiled at Phoebe as soon as she saw her.

'Is Andreas in?' Phoebe felt like a schoolgirl as she asked the question.

'Phoebe? He is out, I'm afraid.'

'How did you know my name?' Phoebe asked, surprised.

'Not so many beautiful English women come knocking at our door, and Andreas has told me about you. Come in and wait, I don't know how long he will be, he has taken Lefteris to the hospital for an X-ray. I will make us some coffee. I'm Alexa, by the way.'

Alexa showed Phoebe through the darkened ground floor room to a door onto the terrace. From there the view was stunning, looking out onto the village and beyond, down a valley veiled in olive groves heading towards the bay of Mirabello somewhere in the distance.

'It is gorgeous. We are very lucky.' Alexa excused herself and went back inside the house leaving Phoebe alone to take in the dazzling scenery. She emerged again and put a tray of two cups of coffee and a jug of water and glasses on the table. 'I am so pleased to meet you. I know already that we will be friends.'

Phoebe felt relief at how comfortable she already felt in Alexa's company and as they sat and talked, the young Greek woman explained how two days earlier, Andreas' son had fallen and broken his wrist. That was when she had phoned Andreas. Today he had taken Lefteris back to the hospital to check if the bones were realigned.

'I am sorry I had to phone when I did, but as you'll appreciate I had no choice. Did he not tell you what happened?' Alexa asked.

'He must have been too preoccupied worrying about Lefteris.'

'That is no excuse,' said Alexa. 'Andreas is a kind man and a great father. But since my sister died he has found it difficult to rebuild his life. He is scared that if he finds someone else, he will be dishonouring the relationship he had with my sister. From the way he talks about you, this is the first time he has felt relaxed with another woman.' She sighed and continued. 'He has had a hard life, never knowing his parents and then losing his wife when the children were so young. He deserves some happiness but is afraid to grab the opportunity to move on. I don't know if he worries what the kids or me or other people might think, but he will never know unless he…'

'Phoebe. What are you doing here?' Andreas stood in the doorway to the terrace, carrying his son in one arm and holding the hand of his young daughter.

Phoebe felt her heart thudding in her chest. What would Andreas think of her seeking him out at his home?

'I came to find you. Alexa kindly invited me in to wait. Aren't you going to introduce us?'

'I'm sorry, I've forgotten my manners.' Andreas carefully lowered his son into a chair as, released from his grasp, the little girl ran to Phoebe cuddling her knees.

'Are you Pappa's girlfriend?'

Alexa laughed as she translated the girl's words.

'Sofia. Don't be so rude to our guest.' Andreas reddened as he managed to get out his words. 'This is my friend Phoebe.'

'Hello Sofia, hello Lefteri. I'm pleased to meet you.' Phoebe introduced herself.

The two children glanced at each other. 'You speak funny,' giggled Sofia.

'Phoebe's from England,' said Alexa.

'Where's England? I like England. I like Phoebe.'

'I think you have a fan.' A smile broke across Andreas' serious expression.

'I thought I had one already?' Phoebe couldn't help but smile.

'You do. And I'm sorry. I should have explained things to you.'

'So do you and, yes you should.' Phoebe turned to Lefteris. 'And you are very brave.' As his father translated her words to his son, Lefteris' face lit up. Phoebe crossed to where the boy sat and wrapped her arms around him.

Lefteris said nothing, but his smile spoke for him as he sank into the English woman's warm hug.

'Who'd like some food?' Not awaiting a reply, Alexa made her way inside to the kitchen as Phoebe answered a barrage of questions from the children, asked via their father.

Alexa brought two plates of chicken souvlaki and chips for the children and a jug of wine and glasses for Phoebe, Andreas and herself. 'I will get us some food later, when the children are in bed. It's been a long day at the hospital so they must be tired.'

'Will you be here in the morning? Please,' asked Sofia, taking her last mouthful. Andreas blushed almost as much as Phoebe as he translated her question. 'Sofia, you shouldn't ask such things.'

'Come on kids, time for bed I think. Say goodnight.' Alexa said standing.

Sofia hugged Phoebe. 'Please come and see us again,' she said as Alexa took her hand and Andreas bent down to pick up his son to take them inside.

'Goodnight Lefteri, I hope your wrist gets better soon. Goodnight Sofia,' said Phoebe gently.

Alone on the terrace Phoebe sat reflecting on the events of the day as the sun went down. Inside she could hear the murmurings of Andreas and Alexa preparing the children for bed. The clearness of the sky echoed the silence as the weak twinkling of the first stars penetrated the ensuing dusk. As the sun disappeared, Andreas and Alexa joined her.

'Are they asleep already?' asked Phoebe.

'Lefteris is, and Sofia will not be far behind him. They are both tired, but a bit excited to have such an exotic visitor from a foreign land,' Andreas replied. 'And so am I.'

'I don't know about being exotic, but whatever they think, I think your children are lovely,' said Phoebe.

'Not always,' Andreas said, smiling, as he took the compliment on his kids' behalf. 'I think you were a hit with them as well.' He paused. 'I'm pleased you met them... and that you came to find me.'

'I will go and get us something to eat,' said Alexa disappearing indoors.

'I'm pleased I found you too.' Phoebe recalled the events of the day, how she had discovered the address on the honey pot and had taken flight when she had seen Andreas with Alexa and the children. 'It was stupid of me to jump to conclusions.' Phoebe looked down. 'And if Stella hadn't told me about your wife, I might have packed up and moved on and never seen you again.'

'I'm sorry, Phoebe. It was me who was foolish. I was afraid of introducing someone new into our family. I was confused and scared to take the next step. Now you have done that for me.' Andreas bent down and kissed her. 'Thank you for finding me,' he whispered in her ear.

Phoebe found herself welling up. Tears of joy and relief ran down her cheeks. Sniffing she drew back from Andreas and thought she saw a glistening in the corner of his eyes too.

'I'll get you a tissue.' Andreas turned his face away and disappeared, before returning, composed, and handing Phoebe a paper napkin.

Coming out onto the terrace with a bowl of salad and only two plates of chicken souvlaki and chips, Alexa excused herself saying she had a headache, was tired and needed an early night. Andreas lit a candle lantern and placed it between himself and Phoebe on the table. Their appetite for the delicious meal almost matched their need to open up to each other about the past.

Andreas revealed how he had been brought up by a friend of his father's following his parents' death. He spoke lovingly about the man who had cared for him, who he had always considered his *baba* or dad. His childhood had been a happy one spent in Rethymnon where his *baba* provided for them by teaching and playing the lyra. When arthritis set into his fingers and he could no longer sustain the rigours of regular performance, his *baba* had made a living writing songs for other musicians which led him into a career as a successful music producer in Athens.

Andreas disliked the restlessness of the big city and, when he was old enough, made his return to the hillsides of Crete where he had discovered his passion for keeping bees. He had been 35-years-old when he married a girl from Kritsa and thought life could not get any better. Her father had given them the house in the village before he died and with it came the right to put his hives on the land in Katharo. It took some time before the children Andreas longed for were born, but their births made the family complete.

Life was turned upside down when his wife found out she had cancer and she died just months after the tragic diagnosis. Andreas had been devastated, and with the help of his sister-in-law Alexa had drawn a protective ring around his young family and put on a brave face to the outside world. Now his bees had taken on a greater importance in his life, the clearing on the plateau being a place to which he could escape to find the solitude he sometimes needed to cope with his grief.

Andreas had never opened up to anyone other than Alexa before about his past, and telling Phoebe his story, he felt the burden he had been carrying for so long fall from his shoulders. He became aware that he had been talking of his own life for much of the evening and encouraged Phoebe to let him in to the story of how she had come to Crete.

She told how she had followed her mother into a career in music but how that career had fizzled out after she had got married and her happiness had turned to sadness as their attempts to have a family all came to nothing and ended in the acrimony of divorce. Phoebe opened up about how she had tried to rebuild her life but however hard she tried had been unable to feel whole, and how her mother had encouraged her to visit Crete to try and experience the culture that had given birth to half of her being.

'And your father gave the bee pendant to your mother, who gave it to you, and that led you to me,' Andreas said. 'We are meant to be together.'

Chapter 13

TOUCHING DOWN IN Athens, Liz reflected on how it was the first time she had been to Greece since Georgios had been arrested and she had been thrown out of the country. Now she was back to celebrate the wedding of their daughter. Her joy that Phoebe had found happiness pushed any anxiety she might otherwise have experienced to the back of her mind. Looking at her watch she noted there was nearly an hour to wait before Anna's plane from Australia landed.

It had been only a month ago that she had been reunited with Anna. She was shocked when she received a friend request on Facebook from Georgios' sister, who had recently been encouraged by her grandchildren in Australia to sign up and had searched for

Liz's name. If Liz had been surprised to hear from Anna, it was nothing to what Anna felt at the news that she was an aunt.

Finding each other again had brought to the fore so many memories for both women. When Liz asked if she would like to attend her daughter's wedding as a surprise for Phoebe, Anna also swept aside any doubts she might have had of returning to the island which she fled in such anguish more than forty years before.

The anticipation of seeing her friend again after so many years was almost too much to bear. Liz had a coffee to while away the time, but the hands of her watch seemed to be going in slow motion. She tried to read her book but could not get the words to stick. She settled for watching strangers passing through the gate and glancing at the screens to see if Anna's flight had landed.

Emerging from the arrivals gate, Anna was swaddled in a hug from Liz, both women tearful with emotion at their reunion. Despite the passage of time and the challenges life had brought them, the years had been kind to the friends. In each other's eyes they were reminded of the bond that had been forged between them all those years ago. Although they had only known each other for a few days back in the dark times of the Junta, their friendship was instantly rekindled. Wheeling their cases to the domestic departure check in, they fell into animated conversation as though trying to make up for all the lost years. They had two hours before their connecting flight to Heraklion.

An angry crowd surrounding the desk was the first sign that all was not well. Their fears were confirmed when they looked up at a screen to the announcement that all domestic flights that day had been cancelled due to industrial action. Their options were limited. They might still be able to make the wedding if they could catch the overnight ferry from Piraeus to Heraklion. Searching the internet on her phone for a number, Anna called to try and book tickets but, with no flights going and it being the height of the tourist season, there were none available.

By the time they had reached the front of the queue at the airline desk, the first flight the beleaguered woman could offer them was at noon the following day. The wedding was at 11 o'clock so there was no way they could make it to the ceremony. There was nothing they could do. Distraught, they resigned themselves to accept the tickets.

*

When her mother called from Athens to tell her the news, Phoebe could not hide her disappointment. Until that moment she could not have imagined life to be more perfect since Andreas' proposal just a month after her first visit to the house in Kritsa. He had asked her to marry him over dinner in a waterside taverna in the village of Mohlos as they looked out on a small island just offshore while the sun set on the mountains above like a Monet painting. As a gift, Andreas had presented Phoebe with a pair of earrings to match the bee pendant given to her by her mother.

The following weeks had gone past like a whirlwind as they made the necessary arrangements for the ceremony and reception, and got all the documentation needed to tie the knot. As it was second time around for both of them, the couple agreed they did not want an extravagant wedding and had planned for the ceremony to be held in the church of Panagia Odigitria in Kritsa. Stella had offered to host a reception afterwards at the café at her villas where Phoebe was still staying. Liz was Phoebe's only family and she had not been able to mask her own upset about not making the ceremony. She took the directions to Stella's café at the villas where she had also rented a room, and promised to make every effort to get there for the reception. Andreas managed to console Phoebe, reminding her she would still see her mother, and that when she arrived she would forget she had not witnessed the service in the church.

Seeing her mother would make her happiness complete. It was her mum who had encouraged her to come to this island where she had found love and a family in a beautiful place where she felt whole and so at home. Phoebe knew her mother would do everything she could to get to the reception.

Andreas had been right: as soon as the priest began the ceremony, the blessing of the rings, the vows and the promenade around the church all went by in a flash. Emerging into the light, they took time for some photographs before the small convoy of cars headed down the mountain. As they drove, people stopped to wave and other drivers honked their horns to congratulate the newly married couple making their way to the coast.

For Andreas, his sister and the children, it had been a tearful reunion with Andreas' *baba* when he had flown in from Athens two days before. Now the elderly man was squashed into a car alongside Alexa, Lefteris and Sofia, the adults hardly less excited than the children at the prospect of the impending celebrations.

'What's that?' Sofia pointed at the case her granddad cradled in his arms.

'That's my lyra. That reminds me.' Reaching into the pocket of his jacket, he took out a packet of pills, popping two from the foil wrapper and swallowing them.

'I promised myself I would play at Andreas' wedding, and these help ease the pain in my hands so I can play for a short time before they seize up again.'

'Andreas will love that,' said Alexa. 'I remember you playing at my sister's wedding.' A dark veil fluttered through her thoughts at the memory of the children's mother. 'It was perfect.'

'We all miss her.' Alexa felt a comforting arm around her shoulder. Holding back the tears she turned her face to the window so the children could not see her distress. Looking down she could see the sun-bathed bay of Korfos, the causeway winding towards the canal and in the distance Spinalonga floating like a mirage in the distance. Sniffing, Alexa let the beauty drift over her, and found the will to return her thoughts to the happiness the day would hold.

Andreas held the car door open for his bride and, stepping out, she looked around for her mother. Letting go of Alexa's hand the children rushed towards Phoebe and Andreas, crying out with excitement. The café had been draped with bunting of the blue and white flags of Greece and as soon as Stella stepped from her car she was giving directions to the staff she had hired to help with the reception.

Crisp linen cloths dressed the tables which were soon filled with jugs of wine and dishes of every imaginable mezze. On a raised section in the corner of the terrace, a trio of musicians were already drinking, chatting and adjusting the tune of their instruments.

Phoebe looked again for her mother, but she was nowhere to be seen. She put her hand to her neck, where beneath her wedding dress the bee pendant her mother had given her lay hidden.

'Would you like me to ask Stella to wait before she starts serving the wedding feast? I'm sure she wouldn't mind.' Andreas could tell Phoebe was longing for her mother to arrive.

'No, it's fine.' Phoebe answered. 'I don't want to mess about with Stella's preparations. I'm sure she will get here.'

'She will.' Andreas squeezed her hand as they stood on the steps to the café to welcome their guests. The bride and groom were led to a circular table set aside for close family and friends. As they sat, Phoebe watched the trickle of cars of the late arrivals driving along the causeway, over the stone bridge and past the disused windmills. A caique passed through the canal, the fisherman at the tiller blasting his air horn and waving.

The musicians fed, they picked up their drinks and made their way to the podium. Phoebe had been nervous about her first dance with her new husband and they had not practiced. As they took the floor, she was relieved to discover his dancing was just as improvised as her own. As they danced, her view spun from the sparkling bay to the blooming gardens and the laughing guests around them. Phoebe's heart felt as though it could break with joy as she saw Lefteris and Sofia swinging each other round in circles.

Elated and relieved, Phoebe and Andreas returned to their seats, and the dance floor was taken up by guests keen to demonstrate their prodigious dancing skills. Phoebe had met Andreas' *baba* on the evening of his arrival on Crete and was much taken with the kindly man who her husband looked on as his father. As the wine flowed the atmosphere on the terrace relaxed. Now Phoebe found herself sitting next to the elderly man nervously clutching an instrument case.

'Are you alright?' Phoebe enquired.

'I made a promise to myself that I would play for Andreas and his bride at his wedding. I did it for his first marriage and now I want to do it at your wedding but I worry that my fingers won't work the way they used to. I don't usually play anymore.'

'That's so kind of you. You must play. I know you'll be fine; and it will mean a lot to Andreas.' Phoebe rested her hand gently on his shoulder.

The music stopped. 'Georgios!' A musician shouted from the stage interrupting Phoebe. Clapping encouragement he enjoined Andreas' *baba* to take the stage.

'I think they want me now,' said Georgios. 'Wish me luck.'

Bending to take his lyra from the case, when he stood Georgios looked taller than before and as he made his way through the guests towards the stage, Phoebe thought he shed years with every step.

On the podium, Georgios rested the lyra on his knee and the room fell silent. Raising his bow, he drew it across the strings, a long haunting note escaping, flying over the bay of Korfos and through the valleys and echoing off the mountains that surrounded them. As he played, he weaved together notes which at once became part of the very fabric of the landscape that surrounded them. In the man's eyes Phoebe could see a glow she had not noticed before and as he played she felt she had never been so satisfied with her place in the universe. Almost unnoticed he wound up the tempo until the guests found it impossible to keep quiet, clapping and calling out encouragement. They became one with the music as though it had absorbed them into a collective soul which had sprung from the earth.

Georgios made his way back through the cheering guests, ignoring their pleas to play more. As soon as he had finished, he felt his hand stiffen. When he sat down, Phoebe leant over and released the lyra from Georgios' grasp, putting it carefully back into its case.

'Thank you. I will never forget that,' Phoebe said truthfully.

'Thank you for making Andreas so content. But now it is your turn.' Georgios said to a puzzled Phoebe.

'Andreas told me that you are a musician, so you must play. It is a gift that you have been given, so you must share it with your new family and friends.'

'You must play,' Stella implored. 'I'll go to the villa and get your guitar.' Not waiting for an answer her friend left the table.

'Please play, it would mean a lot to me.' Andreas squeezed his wife's hand before crossing the room to speak to the band, which was bravely trying to follow on from Georgios' display of virtuosity.

Whether it was nerves or excitement, Phoebe could feel her hands shaking as she unclipped her guitar case which Stella had placed beside her, whispering, 'You do not stop being an artist. It holds you for life.'

The memory of arriving at the villa in Elounda came back, and with it an awareness of how she had come so far in just a few months. A fragile confidence rose within her as she stood. Grasping her guitar with one hand she reached for the necklace around her neck, pulling the pendant out from beneath her dress, and made her way to the stage.

Alone on the podium she felt her new-found confidence draining from her. But there was no going back. She took a moment to check the tuning of the guitar, then another to look out across the water and at the mountains which towered above the bay. Taking a deep breath she drew her fingers across the strings; she had not even decided which song she would play. Where the opening chord had come from she did not know, and she began a song she had not played for many years, which had been forgotten in the mists of her memory.

If Georgios' playing had reached into their souls, Phoebe's voice and guitar tugged at the heartstrings of the guests and they sat in silence as her words found an emotional connection. Phoebe sensed the reaction of the audience and gained confidence. Looking at the table she saw the pride on Andreas' face as she played. Then her glance fell on Georgios. He was standing, his eyes wide and mouth open as he started towards the stage.

As Phoebe played the last note the guests erupted with applause and it took time before she could hear what Georgios was trying to say to her.

'Where did you learn that song?'

'My mother wrote it as a love song for my father before he died.'

'Georgios!' The elderly man turned as two women called his name in unison. He couldn't believe what he was seeing.

'Mum, you made it!' Phoebe jumped from the stage to hug her mother but before she could wrap her in her arms she saw her mother was not looking at her, but at Georgios. She was pulled up short by Liz's words.

'Georgios. I thought you were dead.'

Phoebe stood rooted to the spot; she could not believe what she was hearing.

Tears welled up in Liz's eyes, as for the first time in more than forty years she felt the strong arms of Georgios embrace her. In that moment, Anna's face crumpled before she joined in the emotional clinch.

When Georgios released his grip, Liz stepped back and turned to her daughter, taking hold of her hand.

'Phoebe, this is your father.'

This time it was Georgios who was struggling to contain his emotions as he held open his arms to hold the daughter he never knew he had.

With the band still silent, Phoebe could make out the murmurings of the guests, who were trying to make sense of the unfolding drama. She struggled to take in what was happening herself. All she knew was that she was overwhelmed with happiness.

Stella signalled to the band to play and brought seats for Liz and Anna as they made their way back to the table. In one extraordinary day, Phoebe had married the man she loved, gained a family, and met the father she had long thought to have been dead. Andreas could not believe what he was hearing, that the man who had rescued him from the orphanage in Rhodes was his new wife's father. Across the table, both Liz and Anna were beaming, holding hands and deep in conversation with Georgios. Out on the old stone jetty Phoebe could see Alexa skimming stones with the children as Stella bustled amongst the guests replenishing the tables.

Taking Phoebe's hand, Andreas steered her into the gardens. In each other's arms, their silence spoke of the unquenchable joy they both felt as they peered through the scented blooms at the water gently lapping the shoreline. Phoebe wondered at the timeless quality of this land and the forgotten song which had led her to discover the father she thought had died, and how the pendant he had given her mother had brought her to Andreas.

At the table Liz, Georgios and Anna were desperate to make up for lost time and tell the stories of their lives since the night in Rethymnon which ripped them apart. Liz and Anna listened in horror to the story of Georgios' imprisonment and torture. How he had promised to take care of Andreas and had returned with the baby to the village only to discover his family had left. Unable to face the pain of the memories he had gone back to Rethymnon to earn a living with his lyra but, as he got older, the damage done to his hands and arms made playing for long periods as painful as the memories he held of the night he had been arrested and separated from the woman he loved.

Hoping to find a market for his song writing, he moved with his young charge to Athens, where he made a living selling his tunes to the many artists who played in the boites, bars and clubs in the city. With the resurgence of rebetika following the demise of the Junta he found his experience much in demand and slowly made a name producing artists for the burgeoning new recording market.

Liz relayed the story of her deportation from the country and how she had discovered she was pregnant with Georgios' baby. She told of being unable to contact his family who had fled the country and of the letter from his friend in the village saying that he had died in custody. She fondly related stories of Phoebe's childhood and proudly told Georgios of his daughter's promising career in music which had, over time, fizzled out.

Thinking her brother had died, Anna and her family had found the grief unbearable and the death of Stelios would no doubt have made them a target for reprisals by the fascist forces. They had fled the country, finding refuge with a cousin of Anna's father in Australia. Here the family had worked hard to rebuild their lives and Anna had eventually found happiness, marrying and having two children who were now grown up and had children of their own. Anna could see the sadness on her brother's face when she told him that their parents had only recently passed away within months of each other.

These stories were exchanged as if it had been no more than a day since they had all seen each other. As darkness fell, more space was cleared in front of the stage and the music and dancing went on late into the night. When asked, Phoebe found herself pleased to perform again and even Georgios cajoled his fingers to play one last tune. At the end of the evening, Alexa and Georgios left with the children by taxi for the house in Kritsa. Liz and Anna were shown by Stella to the house they were sharing.

Whilst they had been celebrating, the doorway to Phoebe's villa had been decorated with balloons and the bed scattered with scented petals, pink, red and blue. As the music stopped and the last revellers departed, the only sound to be heard was the gentle sighing of the water caressing the sand beneath the balcony of the newlyweds' room.

*

Looking down over the scorpion village, Georgios slowly turned the spit, stopping occasionally to baste the lamb he was roasting with sprigs of rosemary cut from the hillside dipped in olive oil. The children ran in and out of the house, excited as they waited to see their father and Phoebe, while Alexa prepared a feast in the kitchen.

The events of the day before had given an added air of expectation to the meal Alexa had offered to host. As he tended to the burning coals, Georgios was bursting with excitement at seeing Liz again. As soon as he had set eyes on her the previous day, the years had fallen away and he was taken back to when they had first met, before their lives had been turned upside down.

In her hurry to get to her daughter's wedding, Liz had not had a chance to take in the exquisite views she remembered from her first visit to Elounda all those years ago. That morning, crammed into the hire car with Phoebe and Andreas, she could gaze out at the panorama which unfolded as Anna navigated the vehicle up the mountain road. She could barely wait to see Georgios and, despite the previous night's celebrations, she felt like a young woman again.

When Anna had discovered Liz on Facebook, she could never have imagined it would lead to this. Not only had she found her friend and gained a niece but she had been reunited with the brother she adored and thought had been killed at the hands of the Junta. As she drove, she thought of the lost years they could have had together and tried to reconcile them with happiness she had found in Australia which had only happened because of those tragic events. A smile came to her lips as the car reached the summit and the bay of Mirabello was unveiled in front of them. The sea was blue as enamel and she could remember the awesome beauty of the landscape when she was a girl. The view was unchanged, still having the power to lift her soul.

Looking out of the window, Phoebe pondered the delight this land had brought her. She clutched the hand of her husband, her eyes glowing at the prospect of seeing her father and the children. The car was silent with the thoughts and hopes of the four passengers as they expectantly made their way towards Kritsa.

Parking on the street, they made their way up the narrow lane to Andreas' house. A lizard scuttled for the safety of a crack in a wall as a cockerel crowed from somewhere up the mountainside. Before Andreas reached for the door it was flung open by Alexa, and the children rushed out to be lifted one in each arm by their father.

The aroma of lamb roasting drew them onto the terrace. Georgios hugged each one of the arrivals to convince himself he had not dreamed the events of the day before. Alexa brought out a bottle of champagne and popped the cork to raise glasses to the newly married couple, followed by toasts to Liz, Anna and Georgios. Phoebe looked around, taking in the blossoms of every colour busting from containers and the silver olive trees in the valley beyond. By her side was the man she hoped to spend the rest of her life with and playing beneath the table the children she had so longed for. When she had escaped to Crete she had hoped that visiting the island could fill the void in her soul left by the death of her father. She had now discovered him alive and her heart was bursting with happiness.

Georgios was keen to talk as he returned to turning the spit. He had half a lifetime of news to catch up on. He listened as Liz and Phoebe spoke of their life in England and about their musical careers, which for neither of them had quite taken off. To him, Liz had not changed since the day they had first met that Easter in the village, and Phoebe was a gift of that glorious time they had spent together.

Over the sumptuous lunch, Liz fell into conversation with her daughter and her new husband as Anna immersed herself talking with her brother and Alexa. The table cleared, they sat drinking wine and relaxed into the conversation as though they had been in each other's company for years. High above, the sun dropped towards the mountain tops, burnishing the brown stone to bronze. Alexa lit the candle lanterns, putting one on the table and the others on the terrace wall.

Beneath them a church bell solemnly tolled, echoed by the sound of a spoon on Georgios' wineglass as he stood.

'I would like to say a few words.' Clearing his throat he began to speak. 'These last days have been the happiest of my life. To see the boy I have thought of as a son find happiness one more time with this beautiful woman who is my daughter, to meet her mother again and be reunited with my sister is a gift from God. If I die now, I will be a blessed man.' He paused, then laughed. 'Don't worry, I don't intend to. I have so much left to live for now.'

'Phoebe. Andreas. Your aunt Anna and I have been talking. We would like you to accept as a present our mother and father's house and olive grove in the village. As they all thought I was dead, they left it to Anna. She has no use for it having a home in Australia, and although she kindly offered it to me, I have my apartment and still some work in Athens.'

Andreas and Phoebe could not believe what they were hearing. They had expected to stay in Kritsa for the time being with Alexa, but it would be a bit small now that there were five of them.

'I suspect it needs some work after all these years empty, but the olives should bring in a good income and the groves will accommodate your hives and maybe more.'

The answer to Georgios and Anna's kind offer was agreed in a single glance between the couple. 'Thank you!' they echoed one another, both trying to take in the generous gift.

The following day they all took the journey to the village. For Anna, it was the first time she had been back since she had fled from there with her parents, and Georgios had not been back since the day he had returned with Andreas in his arms. In Liz's head it conjured up memories of the night she had first met Georgios. As he stooped to find the key, still under the stone beside the door where he had left it all those years ago, she saw in him the same man she remembered that night. No one saw her face colour as Georgios handed the key to Andreas, who struggled to turn it in the lock. It yielded, and the door swung open, letting in light for the first time in more than forty years. As they opened the shutters, motes of dust fluttered, reflected in the sunlight as they hovered in the air alongside the memories that came flooding back to Georgios, Anna and Liz.

A breeze blew through the house as Anna opened the back door, clearing the air as they stepped out onto the terrace. They looked down the hillside and saw that the gnarled olive trees looked manicured and well kept; it seemed as though over the years the neighbours had been tending them and harvesting the crop. The shutters and doors that had been open to the elements were weathered and worn and the whitewashed walls stained with the marks of time, but the inside of the house was remarkably well preserved, if in need of a major clean. In a bedroom, a drawer from a chest lay on the floor, reminding Georgios of the day he had returned when Andreas was a baby to find the house abandoned. Since then nobody had crossed the threshold.

Immediately Phoebe felt at home, she adored the house. Already Andreas was enthusiastically making plans for how he would decorate and renovate the outdated kitchen and bathroom. The vine which covered the pergola on the terrace was still flourishing and bunches of mature grapes hung, waiting to be picked. In the pots and containers most of the plants had died, but through the cracks in the walls wild geraniums and a fig tree flourished and a bougainvillea had grown huge, covering the whole of the back wall and creeping around the sides of the house.

The children excitedly ran in and out of the building arguing about who would have which bedroom. There was enough room for them to have a choice with plenty of space for the young family and a room left over for guests to stay. The adults walked inside and out, Phoebe and Andreas making plans and Georgios and Liz lending suggestions. Only Alexa was quiet. She had taken herself into the olive grove and was deep in thought in the shade of the old trees.

'How selfish of me. I'm sorry.' Andreas' words shook her from her reverie.

'I didn't hear you coming.' Alexa turned. 'Why sorry? For what?'

'All this talk of us moving, with no consideration for you and the house in Kritsa. It was thoughtless. We would like you to have it.'

'Have what?'

'The house, you must have the cottage in Kritsa. After all it was your parents who gave it to your sister and me. We do not need it now and you have helped me so much since she died. I would like you to have it, on one condition.'

Alexa looked incredulous. 'Thank you, thank you. Of course.'

'Don't you want to know the condition?'

'I know already. The bees.'

'You know me too well.' Andreas laughed. 'I will set up more hives here, but you will now have the rights to the hives on Katharo, so I will tend them for you and we can go into business together selling the honey.'

Alexa's first thought had been that she would miss Andreas, Phoebe and the children. But it was not far to the village, and as things sunk in she realised she had found a new freedom. Not only had she been given a house, but also an income to live off. Although she had never said anything to Andreas and she loved the children, their care had to an extent put her own life on hold. She would not have had it any other way, but now felt the liberation of her future opening up before her.

There were only four more days before Anna had to return to her family in Australia, and Liz to her house in England. Georgios still had work commitments in Athens and would join them on the flight there. They threw themselves into cleaning, painting and gardening at the house in the village. Phoebe sanded the doors, window frames and shutters before painting them blue. Andreas climbed a ladder, filling cracks in the walls before recoating the outside brilliant white. Meanwhile on the terrace, Georgios cut, pruned and planted until it resembled the vibrant oasis he remembered from his youth as his sister and Liz busied themselves making the inside homely.

By the evening before Liz, Georgios and Anna were leaving, the house had returned to its former glory. As the family sat on the terrace, for the older members it brought back memories of their youth spent in the village and for the others hope for the future. The happiness they had discovered in reunion was suffused with the sadness of their impending separation. As they talked they made plans, Anna promising to bring her family to visit Greece; and it came as no surprise when Liz announced that she was staying on in Athens with Georgios for another week before returning home.

With Alexa working with Andreas, they too would see each other regularly.

As the sun sank the mood lifted, thoughts of the past banished as the stars came out one by one. As Phoebe looked up, a shooting star blazed its course across the sky. She had never felt more rooted to her place on the planet. No longer did she feel a void in her soul. When she felt Andreas take her hand, she had never felt more complete.

*

The week Liz had planned to stay with Georgios in Athens had turned into months, and when she returned to her home in Wiltshire, it was as a married woman. The years had not diminished the love the couple felt for one another and they were determined not to waste any of the time they had left together. They spent their life moving between the house on Salisbury Plain and Georgios' apartment in Athens, and frequently travelled to Crete to visit Phoebe and Andreas.

It had been on one of these visits that Georgios suggested they record the song Liz had written for him and through which he had discovered his daughter. It was decided that Phoebe would sing and play guitar, with Liz also playing guitar, and an English musician Sarah, who Phoebe had recently befriended, providing accompaniment on the fiddle. Phoebe also put down an additional track on piano and Georgios recorded and mixed it all on his laptop.

The result of their endeavours was posted on the internet, along with the story of the 'Forgotten Song', and something in its haunting melody and message of love and hope for the future struck a chord in the uncertain times people were experiencing.

When Liz delivered the news of the song's success, Phoebe did not feel the rush of excitement she might have experienced in her youth, but a warm sense of fulfilment that she had quietly achieved what years ago she had longed for. As Liz put down the phone, Georgios took her in his arms, kissing her, and whispered in her ear, 'If you are a musician, you are a musician. You can never lose it. It is part of your soul.'

In Crete, as her husband and children congratulated her, Phoebe pondered the power of music and how it had changed her life. She raised her glass. 'To the "Forgotten Song".'

Did You Enjoy this Book?

If you liked reading this book and have time, any review on www.amazon.co.uk or www.amazon.com would be appreciated. My website Notes from Greece is https://notesfromgreece.com, and it would be good to meet up with any readers on my Facebook page at www.facebook.com/richardclarkbooks.

Printed in Great Britain
by Amazon

58654938R00137